T0000172

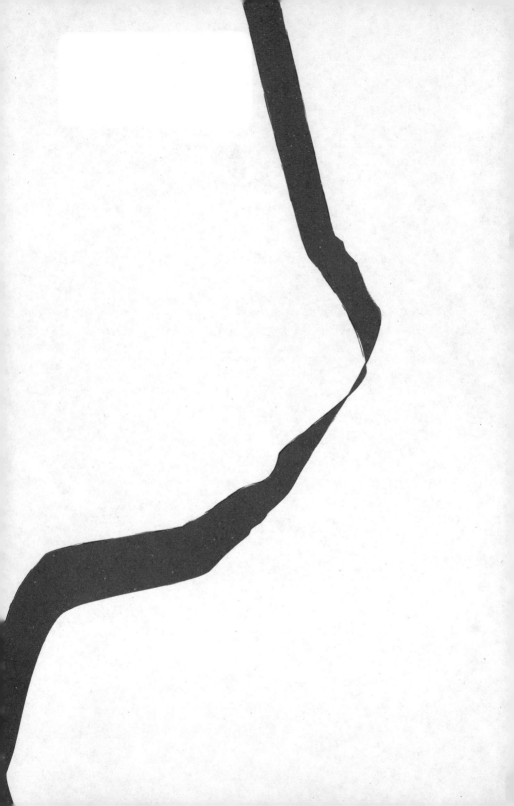

HOUSE GONE QUIET

STORIES

KELSEY NORRIS

SCRIBNER

NEW YORK LONDON TORONTO SYDNEY NEW DELHI

Scribner
An Imprint of Simon & Schuster, Inc.
1230 Avenue of the Americas
New York, NY 10020

Stories in this collection were first published in different form in the following: "The Sound of Women Waiting" (published under the title "An Escalation"), in *The Georgia Review*; "Stitch," in *TriQuarterly*; "Sentries," in the *Kenyon Review*; "Decency Rule," in *The Rumpus*; "Such Great Height and Consequence," in *Black Warrior Review*; and "Go Way Back," in *Midnight Breakfast*.

First Scribner trade paperback edition October 2023

For information about special discounts for bulk purchases, please contact Simon & Schuster Special Sales at 1-866-506-1949 or business@simonandschuster.com.

The Simon & Schuster Speakers Bureau can bring authors to your live event. For more information or to book an event, contact the Simon & Schuster Speakers Bureau at 1-866-248-3049 or visit our website at www.simonspeakers.com.

Interior design by Hope Herr-Cardillo

Manufactured in the United States of America

10 9 8 7 6 5 4 3 2 1

Library of Congress Cataloging-in-Publication Data is available.

ISBN 978-1-6680-1631-2
ISBN 978-1-6680-1633-6 (ebook)

To Alex. To Mom, Dad, and Dave.
To the people I call home.

CONTENTS

HOUSE
GONE
QUIET

THE SOUND OF
WOMEN WAITING

ANA STOOD IN THE COURTYARD of our compound one
afternoon, announcing to all the world her intentions for
her husband. "I can't take it anymore," she said to the air around
her, to all of us. "I'm killing him tonight."

Ana was not a pretty woman, but just then, in the strip of sun
that came through the tattered awning to wrap her in heat and
light—which caught her in such a way that you might forget the
watery nature of her eyes and the way her chin sunk in—she was
almost beautiful.

"He deserves it. They all do," she said with the finality of someone leaving, someone unconcerned with what she left behind. In
that light, you could almost miss the stain of bruising on her arms,
or the desperate way her lip quivered forward. The pockmarks in
her cheeks and forehead seemed suddenly purposeful. "We could
do it, easy," she said. "Soon."

We had to break the spell. We dragged her away from that
beam of light, back into the shadows where we shushed and soothed
her. "You couldn't. We couldn't do that," we whispered into her

hair. "Enough now." Softly, the way our mothers had with us. And then, "Remember home? Tell us about your brother. Saulus? Tell us about the garden." We knew that this would calm her. We held her and listened until she was still. Then we left her there to gather herself, to go on with the life that was left for us.

Her husband was a brute, it was true. He liked to place his hands wherever, however he pleased. Something in his life had made him mean and rotten, or else he simply was—perhaps preferred himself—that way. The women in our building avoided him as best we could. He was the sort of man who made us happy to have our own husbands—who were too tall, too fat; who were meek or unhandsome; who chewed with their mouths wide open and slapped our asses in front of company. Paulo, who couldn't sing and shouted more often than not. Slow, simple Frank who could only run errands for the other guards. Ana's husband made us grateful for every one of them.

We did not choose to live this way—to keep peace with our open legs. The war had finished. Our country had lost so many, so quickly, that it was decimated. Our government threw up its hands, stepped out of the enemy's way. *You've won*, they said. *Take what you will; let us live.* And so we were permitted to live, just barely. First they took what fruits our land could offer up, our freedoms. When this country held out their hands once more, we women were the prize.

The young women of my country are largely considered beautiful. We are thin—slender in a way their women are not. We have seen them, these women, in the photos our husbands show us—their mothers and sisters, the lovers they had before. Where they are padded and soft, we are all sharp edges and corners. It is said that if our women turn sideways, we will disappear entirely, and this is what draws their men to us like ants. We are what they cannot have; or could not. Our country trucked loads of us across the border—as peace offerings, as wives—and what could we do but go?

I refused to leave with the first three waves of women.

"You must," my father told me. "What will we make of you here?"

Though the war began far from us—in cities I never saw before they were only rubble and stone—it radiated outward, until our land was not far from its border. Once the fight was more than rumor, more than young men leaving home to search for glory somewhere at its center, it was the rumble of tanks and torched fields and those young men staying gone.

When we found the bodies of two of our goats twisted and strewn bloody in the garden one morning, my father grew more fervent. "You will leave, Satya," he said, that night and every other night after. He was a hard man whom I had never grown to love. I had a sister, once. A flu took Katarina when we were young, and watching his oldest grow pale and wasted had turned my father mean. Mama told me of the stories he would whisper into my crib—how he moved his hands through the air as he spoke, how she would sneak away and fall asleep, smiling at the tender heart of her husband. But I can only remember him cold.

"Next time they call, you're gone."

What's left for you here? I imagined him saying instead, *We cannot keep you safe.*

He fell asleep by the door most evenings while Mama bustled about, preparing for the coming cold. I stayed up with her, boiling jars clean for canning. We cut okra and beets for pickling, halved pears to pack and cover with syrup. Mama and I didn't speak as we worked but moved around each other in an easy rhythm, maybe hummed as we repeated the familiar steps. That year, a quarter of the jars would go unfilled, as if the earth, too, had been picked dry.

The government recruiter came knocking just before the rest of the goats would go missing. "Your daughter will be happy there," he said. The man sat in our living room, grinning as he spoke, turning his words over so quickly that I knew he believed his own story. "It's a new start for her. These men are not soldiers. They want peace, just as we do. Satya can give us that." He had a bronzed cap over one incisor, which he licked before the start of each sentence. It gave his words a slick, wet sound. "We all have our duty," he said. I remember him winking here, but perhaps he did not.

In the end, I left for my mother. The recruiter said that our country was no longer asking. Paused on our threshold on his way out, he said that each household in the region was required to send half its women. My mother would be finished there, and so the choice was easy. I loved her more than I loved myself.

The government truck that would carry us across the border was so full that the other women and I were made to stand. If we had thought of it then, we might have sat in shifts, some women scooting closer so that the others could rest until the time to trade positions came. Instead, we leaned with the curves and bumps of a broken road we could not see, swaying like one weeping mass of sea grass. Most of the women were my age, though some were young enough to feel chosen, and others were the ages of their brokenhearted mothers.

Later, in the compound, our trip there would not be something we discussed. Pain or shame at the way we were transported like cargo rendered mentioning it taboo. We were simply in one country and then another. But still, I wondered: Had the memory slipped away from the others? Did it haunt them? Was Ana's journey there like mine?

The perfume of the women in the transport and the stink of those who had forsaken any mingled into the same sugary, noxious scent before it became indistinguishable from the air around us. We were strangers and we were all we had.

After some time, when the sniffling of the women had worn down, I felt a sharp pain rip across my scalp. I turned and caught the glint of silver before it disappeared, tucked into another woman's shirt. My mother's barrette, hastily fastened into my hair before the truck pulled away. The barrette now nestled into the fabric cup beneath a stranger's sweating breast. My mother, long hair swirling about her face unchecked as she waved goodbye.

The thief smiled at me. She closed her eyes as if to sleep. She was an arm's length away, and she was safe. There were too many between us for me to reach her. Her nose was bent—crushed and healed crooked sometime before—and I hated her.

I must've cried then. The memory brings a choked, strained feeling to the front of my throat, and yet I cannot remember the tears themselves: how they must have blurred the faces of the women around me and run into the neck of my dress. In that memory there is only the closeness of bodies and the heat and the fear we had all packed into that space with us, the pain at my scalp already fading to numb with every meter of road.

Then, a new pressure in my palm, a parcel tucked into it. A tea bag—the same, simple kind that my family drank most afternoons. A kind of consolation. I squeezed it, and the parched leaves inside rustled and snapped.

"Be strong," a woman behind me whispered into my ear. I did not turn to thank her. I could not, in that cramped and lonely space. She could have been any one of them.

A thick, tinlike sound began to pepper the walls of the truck. Rain struck the caravan, drowning out any chance at conversation, though we had not tried much at all before. Perhaps, then, the men driving grew ashen and nervous. Perhaps, in the cab up front—where they carted us to new lives—their grips grew tighter, knuckles pale. It might've sounded like the racket of wartime. For those of us packed into the back, the sound held comfort. Ignorant as we were of the patter of bullets, we let that deluge fill the silence between us.

Our engagements were quick, efficient. The drivers unloaded us at the border, and we took in all that we could of our new home: smooth pavement without craters or decay, squat buildings, birds that chirped and cawed like ours. The streets packed in closer. Two soldiers in gray uniform led us onto a raised stage in a warehouse where we were made to walk in neat rows, taking turns to pause up front and center. When I was young, I begged my mother to put me into a pageant, but she had refused, citing money or frivolity. And to look at me then! Fit for a crown.

My marriage happened like this: fingertips, pressed into a palm. This is the way the men were told to pick us. They simply had to approach the woman of their choosing, reach up to take her hand, and we were theirs—the whole mess of courting and proposal and matrimony in one brief gesture. When my turn came, I did not immediately look down to see who had chosen me. Eva says that fights broke out over her hand, but I hardly would have noticed such a thing. I was looking for the thief with my mother's barrette, convinced she'd be wearing it now to seem more beautiful. The man who would become my husband was forced to tug at me, to pull me off-balance and slightly out of line before I noticed him.

And even then, I saw only a part of him. My husband's scalp was beautiful. There was a patch—a clearing at the top of his head that looked as if hair had always been absent from it. That smooth skin caught the room's harsh lighting and threw it back to me, softened and newly complex. After, there were his dark, nervous eyes and his build, as if he had been pressed through tubing—slim shoulders and hips and the proportions squat and strange. But first, I had his scalp. One day, I might rub my thumb across that stretch of skull, tracing patterns, divining the measure of him. That a sensation so perfect could exist in a world like ours . . . it almost could have been enough.

How long does a sense of home take to build? How long until a life feels like your own, rather than something you've fallen into?

We tried. After the fear and the anger left us, and news of our country grew scarce, we tried to accept what had come to us. We unpacked our suitcases and stored them. We learned the parameters of our new world—the walk to the grocery, to our husbands' posts. We wrapped handfuls of our skirts around the courtyard spigot to twist it, learned the order for laundry and for hanging clothes on the buckling wire lines that hemmed the compound. We heard nothing of our families but knew we were keeping them safe.

Before she learned of her husband's preferences, the girl we called Baby unpacked the silk bag her mother had tucked into her suitcase. She clasped the hooks and elastic of those lacy underthings around herself one night and lay in wait for her husband's return. When she opened her robe to show him, Baby said the look he gave her was something like pain. He leaned in and kissed her jawline, said, *You're beautiful.* He closed her robe and left again, came home hours later, skin thick with smoke and booze. When he reached for her that night, Baby rolled to him, content at least to know the shape of the life they'd have together.

So there we were, in the courtyard with Ana. In our apartments. In those rooms that we worked to make smell like home, at least. Free for the day of the companions we did not choose but had to lie beside each night. There we were in those hallways, in that country that did not belong to us. Washing, cooking, laughing at times despite ourselves. And waiting, always. Waiting for a thing we couldn't name, but craved.

Do you know what the waiting of three thousand women sounds like?

Nothing. Everything. I'm sure it's something you've heard before.

The report came over the radio one evening: one of our women had killed her husband with a garden tool. The report talked about the blood, her body slumped over his. How spotless the kitchen was otherwise. It called them newlyweds: six months, too short. The authorities had classified it as unintentional. Out of grief over what she'd done, the poor young bride had taken her own life.

In the morning, we whispered that we'd felt our husbands shrink away from us. Their snorts and *Poor bastard*s sounded forced, worried. We felt some hidden suspicion in the language of the report, too—the ambiguity of *garden tool*, a hesitance to name the weapon. We layered our attentions more thickly in the days to come—cooked their favorite foods, kneaded the dip between their necks and shoulder blades. *Trust us*, we meant. We worked a honeyed tone into the tenor of our voices and felt the dumb, blind affection of our husbands return.

We feared what the report would mean to Ana. Her declaration the month before felt like a cracked seal, like a desperate thing finally out in the open. *I'm killing him tonight*, she'd said, though she hadn't. Wouldn't. But now this other woman, this *accident*. We hoped it had not sounded like permission.

She had not always been this way. Ana, who brought a plate of sweets to my door that first week as housewarming and had done the same for each of us. Ana, who had arrived with the first

wave, and whose eyes ricocheted around the spaces of our entry-
ways until we invited her in.

"There's something familiar about you," she told me on that
first meeting, sitting in my living room.

I had tried to hold my face still, tucked a lock of hair more
tightly behind my ear. The other women shook their heads when
they spoke of Ana. They warned me not to get too close. She was
unlucky, they said, for sure. But weren't we all?

"Where did you say you were from?" she asked.

"I didn't," I said. And then, feeling the harshness of that, "Olvyn.
It's very small. My family is still there—my mother and father."

"My father is dead," she told me, flatly, as if she might've said,
instead, *These curtains are the same pattern as mine.* She took a cake
from the plate she had carried to me, chewed it slowly.

It was said that Ana came to us after her first husband died
in some other complex, not so unlike ours. She had been shuttled
farther down the road, passed from that man to another. Even that
first day in my living room, I knew what sort of man her husband
here was. I avoided him.

What had that first one been like? I wondered. Kinder?
Crueler? Just the same?

I waited, and didn't ask. Ana moved the mouthful of cake to
rest in the hollow of one cheek before speaking again. I imagined
it disintegrating as she talked.

On the day she would learn that her father had been killed,
Ana and her mother were cleaning the floors. Her father had cut
the wooden planks himself, fit them over the cold cement of their
foundation. They were proud of the work he'd done. Whenever

guests came for dinner, she told me, they marveled at the russet hue and shine of the floor beneath their feet.

Once, when I was young and ill with a stomach ailment, my mother had given me a horrible mixture to drink in order to force the sickness out. While I vomited into a bin, Mama rubbed my back in circles, murmuring, *Yes, out. All of it, out.* Ana's story had that same necessary quality to it. We all were so broken then, and only half as good at hiding it as we should've been.

She went on, told me that of all the chores she was made to do at home, she liked polishing the floors best. That as she worked away the grime of muddy boots and spills—free of the company of her brothers—she found a stillness that was hard to come by otherwise. They worked crouched on all fours, her mother's knees cushioned but Ana's bare against the wood. When they stood to answer the door, Ana found that the grain had pressed into her skin. She traced those lines with her fingertips as a neighbor delivered the news.

"Papa was dead. Shot," she said to me. "My mother fainted right after." And then, "Have you ever seen anyone faint?"

I shook my head, though I had. I wanted the conversation—its vulnerability—over.

My sister fainted once when we were children, teetered straight forward. The fall was so loud that I thought she must have broken her teeth. I thought that no one could come up whole after a sound like that. I was too afraid to turn her over and see the blood and ruined gums, and so I ran for Mama, who kissed Katarina awake and then pulled me into her arms, too. I watched my sister come back to herself over our mother's shoulder.

I did not tell Ana this. Even then, she was too open, too eager. I knew I could not give what she was hoping for. Later, I held this first image of Ana close: before the vengeance, Ana standing with the veins of a floor stamped into her knees—the imprint there branched and merging, like roots. Ana in my living room, strange but wanting.

In the days after the radio report, Ana spoke to us only of conspiracy. Of our husbands' offenses—the things they had done to us, would do. She plotted strategy and ways of organizing. Didn't the husbands play cards in Mila's apartment every Sunday? What did they eat then? Drink? How many traveled together each morning on their way to the station?

We thought about that woman from the radio, perhaps not so different from us. When we woke in the privacy of our apartments, with memory tangled around our ankles like bedsheets, we felt we understood what she had chosen. We remembered the way our husbands looked at us that evening after the news of what she'd done: as if the prize they'd won might have fangs, hidden away. We wondered if we preferred that look to what had come before it.

On that first night with my husband, he did not try to enter me.

He carried my suitcase up the stairs of our apartment building, shoulders tensed by nerves or nature. He whispered the few comforts and details of our new home that he could think of. He bade me sit at a laminate-top table, then bustled away without taking my coat. He brought me a plate of potatoes and onions that were undercooked, overcooked. Oily. He watched my face. He looked around the room as if this were his first night there, too—the blank walls, the few stains on the ceiling not hidden by shadow. He talked in long, rolling sentences and then stopped altogether. He said, *Can you even understand what I am saying?* Our languages were not so different. He said, *Satya?* He said nothing about the meal I'd picked over. He took my dish from me, placed it in the sink. He was careful not to brush my hands.

He smelled the towel hanging in the bathroom and changed it for another. He closed the door behind me and then lay on the bed, fully dressed. Perhaps he listened to the water running, the faucet susurrus rendered new and mysterious. He folded my side of the blankets down, pretended to be asleep in the sudden light of the bare bathroom bulb. He lay still as I circled the bed and climbed in, fully clothed as well but for my shoes and coat. He rolled slightly to stay perched on the edge of a bed that had grown cupped and worn from the presence of only one body at its center.

He lay stiff for a long while. Perhaps he believed I was sleeping.

My husband crept one foot across the desert slope of the bed. He did this slowly, almost imperceptibly, easing it over for many minutes, maybe an hour. Until he could feel the heat of me. Until he felt the ghost presence of my body—its heat—though not the skin itself. My husband hovered there. He must have calculated, judged the distance between brushing and prodding. Maybe the hair follicles on his biggest toe tensed at the promise of that thrilling contact. He would have felt the harmlessness of his curiosity, its inevitability. Perhaps he thought that one touch would not be enough to wake me and that afterward, his foot could begin the trip back—slowly again or else all at once, wrapped in the guise of some night movement. Perhaps he meant to use the excuse of sleep. My husband struck out toward the ghost form of my calf, my ankle. Found only blankets and air.

My husband whipped his stray foot back and rolled over to face the ceiling. He swallowed, once. Exhaled. Maybe pressed the skin of his eyelids together. Perhaps my husband felt something like anger or embarrassment or the white-hot shame that the opposite sex had brought him so many times in his youth, his adulthood. Perhaps he feared that things would remain as they always had been. He fell asleep in the same way his foot had crept across the mattress—steadily at first, and then gone.

He did not feel the presence of a young wife leaning over him, studying the still-agonized expression across his sleeping face and the way the skin of his neck stretched so thinly that one could almost make out the ribbing of his throat beneath to count the fragile bones there. He could not have felt this.

We left Ana alone. Before the report and her proclamation in the courtyard, we had grown used to looking past her. This happened slowly, almost unintentionally.

Ana brought meals and trays to our doors, and we felt ourselves pause before stepping aside to allow her entry. We offered her a seat at our kitchen tables, and she ventured into our living rooms instead. She lounged in our homes. She told us the same stories, changed the smallest features. She invented concerns for the compound to take on: regulating noise levels, taming the weeds that pushed through the pavement.

She asked us to recount what we remembered of home. Was it greener there? How had the air felt, pressed against our skin? She asked why this country didn't seem to have dogs, if a storm gave more warning here or at home. She wanted details: the size of the pastries we made at holidays, the marbled hues of our siblings' eyes. The patterns of the most beautiful things we had worn, there. We reached back and found these memories slipping. We confused names and faces. Somehow, home had become a dun-colored thing in our minds, and we resented Ana for showing us what we'd lost.

We knew, too, that despite our curt replies and excuses, we were a haven. That Ana came to us because there was nowhere else to go. Seeing her need for us so naked and bare reminded us of the soft wanting that each of us kept hidden, the falseness of the lives we were working at. We spurned her meals, her company, her desire for what we would not give—until the only kindness Ana received came from a cruel husband.

We could not blame her, then, for what she became, for the way she wrung her hands as she plotted around the weaknesses of our husbands. How many compounds were there like this one, strewn along the border? How many wives like us, hoping for a kind of rescue? We didn't know, couldn't tell her. We felt better when her plans included us. Surely her husband was safe while ours were. Surely she wouldn't do such a thing alone.

We felt responsible for such a fragile thing so ruined.

We stalled Ana. We soothed her with small tasks. We calmed

her and had her sit, brought her loose buttons and things that needed mending. We invited her back into our homes and stood beside her at the sink, passing her sopping dishes to dry. We pushed ourselves to recall, to remember: the burst of spices that meant home, the lilt of songs we'd lost.

Once, when the swelling on her cheek was shiny and fresh, I ran my fingers through Ana's hair. I wove the tendrils of her thin strands together, surprised that I still remembered the motions. I shushed her. I pressed the pads of my fingers to the bruise and felt the heat beating through it.

On nights when dulled thuds issued from the confines of her apartment, we worried about Ana's limits. That desperation we skirted but recognized, might it be a fever we could burn out? We began to give her the blood she was asking for.

The chickens that we kept were easiest. Now, when it was one of our turns for a Sunday hen, we asked Ana to wring its neck. The first time that she tried to spin the animal round and round and then snap the base of its skull like a length of rope—like a cracked whip—she lost her grip. Its head slipped through her fingers and the hen went flying. It landed in a heap before the animal stood and ran, dragging its head limply behind it.

We rushed to help her end it. We thought that horrible sight would wreck her. But before we could reach the chicken, Ana caught the head of the animal and sawed it off with a knife that she drew from the seam of her skirt. She cut into the creature again, just above the shoulders so that, now severed, it looked as if the incident had gone as planned. She carried the stretched neck of it away, and we did the same with the body of our Sunday chicken.

We called out to her retreating back, "Ana, the knife," but she continued as if she had not heard. She did not repeat the mistake.

In the letters to my mother, I did not talk about the war. I could not ask about home or the ways that she missed me, and so I told my mother what I thought a marriage was.

Mama, a letter might say, *a marriage is meals shared. It is a whole day recounted over the chime of silverware. It is watching the same face arc in the same way and learning how to glean the feeling there. Marriage is the same meals cooked every week and the compliments despite this. It is the space left when those comments fade.*

Or else, *Mama, marriage is timing. It is mornings and evenings shifting around one another, the waltz of a small bathroom with chipped linoleum and mold showing beneath the tiles. It is two people waiting for each other and then despising that closeness. It is an escalation. A bath mat left dry and unused on the rack and a wet floor. Dishes in the sink. Marriage is finding the fight each time you go looking for it.*

Once, *Today it was a turtle he found and carried back to me. A turtle—here! Even more out of place on our coffee table. Its legs—dry and wrinkled like knuckles—slowly easing out of its shell. Us sitting for an hour, letting dinner go cold. Barely breathing, leaning in. Waiting for it to emerge and then as soon as it did, gathering the turtle up again and flipping it over. My husband's lettering markered on the beige grooves there. Our initials, carried on the underbelly of a living thing.*

The letters might say, *Mama, marriage is rough heels catching the fibers of bedsheets.* Or, *It is the way that he cracks the core of a head of lettuce against the counter so that the leaves fall open.*

I would ask my mother, sometimes, how things had been between her and Papa. I craved a time line. I wanted to know the order of things, how long a feeling took.

It is the way that we like our tea—two sugars; none.

It is the way one might yelp in the shower and how the other can feel the current coming through the water, too. The shock of an ungrounded water heater through torn cuticles, chafed skin.

I folded the letters carefully, setting the creases with a fingernail pressed hard. I ran my tongue across the seal of the envelope, tasted the traces of bitter glue left there.

It is feeling the dip in the floorboards before I step.

It is the way his cheeks smell.

It is, it is.

I let the letters pile up on the edge of the desk and then burned them. This was a stipulation of our place in that country, our agreement with the enemy. A new life, new home. No communication. No reports back. Promises worked into unspoken wedding vows. I never sent a single letter to my mother, but I could not stop myself from writing them.

After Ana's second announcement, and the third, we grew nervous. How long until one of the husbands came home early and heard? How long until they learned our word for *kill*, which was not so different from theirs? We shooed the younger, more impressionable wives away, but they were drawn to Ana, to the prospect of escape. Despite ourselves, we listened too.

Don't you want to leave this place?

Didn't we?

Ana leaned in, spoke to the parts of us that still clung to what could have been. How tall had our brothers grown in the time that we'd been gone? How long until a country's rebuilt?

In another life, Ana might have been a leader. She spun around our complex, urging us to join her. She schemed, collected weapons. After Grace grew sick from tea brewed from a courtyard plant she thought was medicinal, Ana went out into the night and gathered the same leaves.

The accusations against our husbands piled up. They wanted us to stay home, to live half-lives in a country we could not navigate without them. *What kind of man takes his wife prisoner?* The husbands kept us from happiness. Ana repeated the terrible things they called us when their tempers slipped. She'd been listening through our apartment walls, too.

We added to the charges without meaning to. The husbands tracked mud onto the carpets, we admitted. They left stains, complained about the way we kept house. They carried the scent of other women in with them. Those complaints we'd piled away stoked the fire Ana tended. They fucked us loudly, pounding against the headboard so that each man was performing for his neighbor, proving himself. The husbands demanded meat for every meal, then let it gather and wilt in the creases between their teeth.

My mother once said that after they married, my father spent the first years thickening her up. "He was the one that cooked in the beginning," she said, back when our home was still ours. "He made us roasted pig and goat, said it would go to my bones. But it went somewhere else." She had traced the lines of her chest, her stomach, her hips with soft palms. She lifted her hands and shrugged, then went on with dusting the glass figures we kept on display in the cabinet. She ran the rag of my father's old undershirt across the dulled surfaces of hollow swans and angels, and I tried to imagine my mother, my father, as they must have been before.

But *we* did not let our husbands cook. We resisted their attempts to change us, to make us what we had not been before them. My husband brought home a new scarf to replace the one I wore most days—one of my mother's, gone thin and faded at the folds. *You can live better now*, he said to me. I left the gift boxed up on the dresser until he hid it away again.

Ana's indignation began to feel good, like something we could try on. Now, when the husbands swatted at our backsides, we caught their wrists.

With each passing month, her efforts gained focus, though they remained obscure to us. Ana began to spend her days away from the compound, away from where we could watch her. She would return before our husbands did, and in the mornings, slip cryptic messages beneath our doors.

We are not the only ones, the notes said.

Be ready.

But ready for what?

One night, I spotted Ana from my window. In the glow of the last bright, spring moon, I saw her in the courtyard, slumped upon that same makeshift stage as before. I made sure that my husband was sleeping and stepped out, the twisting in my gut something familiar.

When Katarina had been sick for a long time, I would sneak into her room after my parents had fallen asleep. On those nights, I would lean over her sleeping frame to find that she was only ragged, stale breath with a slim face that looked so little like my sister's. Back in my room, I would hope for it to end. In a guilty, dark place inside of me, I prayed that in the morning we would draw the blankets over this Katarina, that we would kiss her fore-head goodbye.

Ana was crouched on the cement platform. She did not stir when I stepped into the light, when I called out to her. Her hair was drawn around her face, and although the strands were nor-mally the color of thin mud, they held the night's silver. I reached to part that light from her face, but Ana drew away.

"No," she hissed.

I stepped back, tucked my hands against my belly. I exhaled the breath I didn't realize I'd held. I looked around and up to the windows that still held light. The silhouettes there—watching as always—stepped away. The wives trickled into the courtyard, fil-tered in at the edges. Some yawned, still rubbing sleep from their eyes. Others fidgeted, nervous that a husband might notice their absence and find us beneath the moon.

"Ana," I tried again.

She straightened her back then, steadily as if lifted by some string. And we waited for her: to deliver whatever rant might satisfy her; to say what she must, quickly, so we could climb back under our cooling sheets. Ana reached up both hands and drew her hair back. She tucked the tail of it into the neck of her nightdress so that we might see.

A new mark shone from her cheekbone. It looked, almost, like a beauty mark she'd been denied, suddenly risen. We drew closer, out of shadow despite the risk, and saw that it was pressed *into* Ana's skin. We saw the puckered lip of the burn, the way it cratered around a center whose color we couldn't be sure of. We hadn't even known he smoked.

We tried to remember the pallor of Ana's legs. Were they smooth? Unshaven? Had she always worn sleeves, or was it only tonight? Was this burn the first, or the first that we had noticed? After we had finished the looking, after we knew the mark for what it was—a sort of brand, now out in the open—our eyes met hers.

Conflicting reports say that she was either broken or proud. Some say that hers was the posture of something cornered, equal parts cower and retaliation. Regardless, we understood then what was at stake. What she was asking of us, perhaps had been asking all along. We might have hung there, held by a current in the air.

Ana nodded her head once and climbed down from her pedestal. She stepped barefoot through the grass, climbed the stairs that would take her back. We followed her, each of us turning a doorknob away from its creak, stepping into an empty living room. In my dreams that night, the men in our compound fell like dominoes, one's blood pooling into another's while a chorus of *Now! Now!* rippled through us like sparks.

When my husband sleeps, it is with one hand reaching toward me. I wake to find it pressed against my stomach. Lately he has begun to broach the subject of children; it has been fourteen months and six days, so this is not wholly unexpected. He has been relatively patient. When he asks, he does so kindly. Carefully. My husband asks for a baby who will look like me, will weave drunken circles around our apartment on new feet, will coo and gaze back at us with eyes that look like his, or mine.

The women of our compound have been careful. Our husbands think we are infertile or cursed or ruined. They believe our slender frames are not built to hold life, or don't do so easily. But accidents have happened. My husband watches these children through the window as they teeter and laugh and fall, and he turns to me with eyes glinting. He tries out names: *Abram? Thea?* When he asks, it comes out like an apology.

When we make love, he places his hands across me as though I am something fragile, and he is gentle with the thin-skinned parts of my body I took months to show him. He was patient then, too. When we make love, the lights are almost always off, because he is ashamed of his shape and the way it looks cupping mine. In the dark, I can imagine he is someone else and that we are different people together. But then I find his eyes boring into mine, trying to communicate through that delicate membrane, and I despise him again.

Vera? Leo?

I have thought of the ways to kill him. How my husband forgets to unplug the portable heater when climbing into the bath, and the ease of puddles. He does not cook; he was ill-suited for it, and I took on the task long before it was strategic. I keep a journal tucked beneath the couch cushions, and in it I record the way he spends his days, the routes he takes to work each morning and then back again to me. I have considered every sharp object in our house, have hidden some in places they do not belong. Even without this, our home is full of danger. Do you know what damage drain cleaner can do to the throat, the organs?

Lucas. Nina.

When I was a child, I watched our village drunk die from drinking antifreeze. He had broken into the shed of a neighbor as he had a thousand times before, but on this night he carried a bellyfull of the solution out with him. I liked him, though my parents warned me to stay away. He was not so vigilant about the distance most adults feel they must maintain with the young. I appreciated the way he spoke to me—all curse words and confession—and how he would lean in afterward to hear mine.

On that night, maybe he wanted to feel warm, or maybe he was looking for a feeling indistinguishable from drunken bliss until it had him entirely. His dying looked like sleeping. The puffs of his breath in the cold thinned to nothing. I watched him go, and kept watching for a time after. I crept from my hiding place to him, then ran home and crawled into bed early, felt my blood thrilling through my veins. It felt good to know a secret. There was power in the knowing and the telling or not telling. Even if the thing was rotten, it was mine.

Katarina.

And now, perhaps there is you. I can feel something growing inside of me, and it is either the slow bud of human life or a mounting anxiety for what we have all become. These are the same feeling, really. If Ana kills her husband, will we follow? If we return home, this band of murderers and runaways and wives, what will we resemble? Would we be welcomed back at all?

If we do not kill our husbands, are we choosing them?

Some of the women remain steady. They leave our compound on errands with Ana and return spirited, more brash. Others have reservations. They have children, or husbands who are caring or mild. For some, life here is kinder than what they left behind. But Ana can feel them waver. She catches these women in the hall or in narrow shop aisles. She tucks her hair behind her ear and leans in, and with that angry indent so close, the women remember their promise to her. We are maybe ugly, broken things. Or else we are magnificent.

Sonia, for my mother.

With each morning that I am sick and my husband leans over me and brings the biscuits he knows I like, the strange mix of pity and excitement in his gaze is unbearable. On those nights, I feel the need to punish him. I watch him sleep and consider his trust spread out beside me—his body, so close. On those nights, I lean in and whisper what truths I can manage into the steady rhythm of his breathing. I tell him about you, about the inkling of you. I try the name *Father* in that space between us. I try the words *dead* and *home*. Only then am I able to sleep.

The way to kill a rabbit is this:

You must catch the animal by its hind legs. It should be fat and slow and will remain nearly docile until the last moment. Hold the legs firmly, but not so firmly as to cause panic. With your other hand, find the meeting of skull and shoulders. It will be a narrow point, where the knobs of bone are the size of rice grains beneath your fingers. Draw your hand back, and then strike with full force at that meeting of spine and skull. The neck will break and the animal will pass without suffering. Do not miss the base of the skull.

In my dreams I am telling this to Ana and she is holding the rabbit all wrong. She grips its legs so tightly that her knuckles are white, and she is smiling and aiming the hard rim of her palm too far down its back. "Not there!" I tell her. "Here!"

At any other point of the spinal column, a striking blow will only break the animal's back, causing it to scream. The sound that a rabbit emits when suffering is high-pitched and loud. Relentless. In my dreams, the cries rise and build up around us even though it hasn't happened yet. The thing is still whole in her hands.

I am reaching out my hand to show her or take the rabbit back, but Ana is pulling the creature closer to her chest. The look in her eye is the surest I've ever seen. She is wrong, and so certain despite this. If you are to break the back of a rabbit, the sound that results is rolling and sharp and thick. Almost human. I am trying to warn Ana about the sound, about all of it, but already she cannot hear me.

STITCH

THEY TALK AROUND THE HORROR. For as long as they can stand it, they talk about stamina, the races they'd been training for, about their weekly mileage, their best split. They talk about their favorite trails and how the foot-give, the quiet, the way the sun crested over the ridge each morning on their last pass brought them peace, accomplishment. A good sweat. They talk supplements—for joint pain or energy or added protein, which goops and bars and shakes give the best boosts. My god, do they miss lactic acid built up in their thighs, waking each morning to soreness before they stretched it through.

There is one barefoot runner, named Jeremy, and they hate him. He is always trying to convert them, saying things like, *Man was born to run this way* and *Terrain is king*, wondering aloud if they can truly know a trail without feeling its rocks and sticks and *features*. Technically, Jeremy doesn't even run fully barefoot, but instead wears swamp-thing Vivos that somehow make him feel superior. He props them up as he pontificates and—subconsciously?—

wiggles each of his separately sheathed, unencumbered toes. They find this unsavory. He wears silky athletic shirts tight enough to see his nipples, which remain unfailingly erect despite a comfortable room temperature.

What they do not bring up until they absolutely cannot avoid it any longer, in the half-lit Dick's Sporting Goods of the Rolling Hills Shopping Plaza, is the reason they stopped running. This—the thing that unites them—brings them back every other week to loiter in the parking lot, to stretch their calves (gone slacker than they'd like) on curbs and bounce on their toes and pitter around, still dressed in running gear, until Stacey, whose boyfriend manages the branch, opens the side door.

Stacey is always already inside, always lets them in as if she runs the place rather than, presumably, a man named Dick, who runs her boyfriend, who runs the place. Stacey lets them inside at exactly 10:00 p.m. Arrive a minute later, and she will refuse to circle back to open the door, leaving the tardy offender locked out and suspicious-looking, wary of triggering the alarm. Stacey says punctuality keeps the devil late.

Once inside, they gather around the miniature running track in the back and sit on benches that employees use to sell shoes in the daytime to customers who won't wear them long enough to push past blisters, and they talk around what haunts them until the pretense runs out. Then they talk about the bodies.

When Sumarra came upon the girl in the woods, her first thought was to leave her. Later, she will not share this with the others, though she wonders if they'd thought the same, finding theirs. It would've been easier, wouldn't it? Simpler.

Sumarra lingered only because she thought the girl might still be alive, the best angle of this worry being that Sumarra could save her and the worst of it being that if the girl did live, she might tell someone about the woman who discovered her first—who came upon a girl leaking into the underbrush—and simply left rather than helping. Sumarra did not like trouble, generally, but made an exception that morning in the woods. She checked her watch to record her pace, then checked the girl's outstretched wrist—which was dirty and alarmingly crooked—for a pulse.

Sumarra was surprised to find that she felt one, at first. The pace matched hers and was strong, jumping slightly from adrenaline, maybe, or fear. She wanted to check the girl's face, to see if her eyes stayed wide or if breath came from her slackened mouth, but the girl's hair was stretched across it, tangled with leaves, and bloodied unencouragingly. Sumarra found a stick to lift the hair away and discovered the source of the blood—which did not seem to be still leaving the girl but instead had already gone—was her head. Her eyes were glassy and grayed, a dulled hazel that might once have been striking. Sumarra checked the wrist again, despite the evidence. She leveled her watch to count out the pace of the girl's impossible heartbeat and realized that she was instead counting her own.

Sumarra cannot remember the next bit, which is what draws her to the support group every other week. She must have called the police. Seven minutes passed between the time that Sumarra last checked her watch to find the only pulse in the clearing and the time she placed the call, a call during which, she's told later, her affect was so flat that the dispatcher asked Sumarra to repeat herself, because Sumarra spoke so quietly, so evenly that the dispatcher could not match what she was reporting with how she said it. Sumarra has not heard the recording and was told by the police weeks after she made it that she was *no longer* considered a suspect. The officer—the detective on the case—had called to tell her this of his own accord, which Sumarra assured herself was normal procedure.

The seven minutes worry her. The call and her supposed affect does not, because how energetic was one supposed to sound about finding a dead girl in the woods, skull ruined but otherwise seemingly intact, barely hidden in a clearing just off the trail, so that someone running by simply had to see it, even if they didn't want to? She can picture the girl as she found her, quite clearly. But Sumarra, who has a firm hold of herself almost always, cannot recall what she did after she realized the girl was dead.

Did she run off, then circle back?

Had she cried? Panicked?

Did she check the girl for further damage?

Had she lain down beside her?

For weeks after the discovery, Sumarra called the station to ask for more details, any evidence they'd found at the scene, which is perhaps why the detective had called her personally afterward, to say she was no longer suspected. He said it was ongoing—the investigation—that he couldn't tell her much, though Sumarra felt that he had anyway: the girl's name, her job, the names of her children, and that her boyfriend had been described by those interviewed as *reserved* and *basically harmless.*

Sumarra let the detective babble on because he needed to, but these were not the details she craved. She did not need to know that the woman—not a girl after all—had run an unlicensed daycare from her home that was clean and bright and much loved by the community. Sumarra did not care that the murder weapon was one of opportunity—that a bit of the rock used to kill her had chipped off inside the woman's parietal lobe, which was the area of the brain most mutilated by the blow. That the parietal lobe was located at the top-middle region of the skull, which meant either that the woman was attacked from behind or that her killer reached over the front of her. That, besides killing her, the blow would have severely impaired the woman's ability to identify objects, would have damaged her spatial reasoning as it related to those objects and herself—as in, the rock and herself, the forest floor and herself, the canopy she found herself gazing into, that open sky and herself. *The parietal lobe is involved in interpreting pain and touch in the body* is the last bit of research Sumarra read before closing her laptop and directing her energies elsewhere.

It does not matter to Sumarra that the blow was dealt by someone strong enough to chip rock inside of someone else, or that the rock was weak enough to break. No, what Sumarra wanted to know was what there was of herself at the crime scene, in the clearing— what pieces of herself Sumarra had left behind, if any, so that she might find them again, or at least understand what was gone.

At this particular meeting, Stacey tells the group that she's been approached by a local station. A reporter wants to do a story for the news about their group, about finder's guilt and its impact over time.

The group bristles at the word *guilt*. Collectively, they bristle. It's an imprecise word for what they feel, for what they feel they're working through. Guilt seems to imply some sort of fault, which is not theirs. It implies a level of participation in the event that they're uncomfortable with, since they were really only participants in its aftermath. *Finder's guilt* seems to imply that the reporter wants sob stories from them—wants them to cry on camera, which would be pathetic, considering that they are not the victims. Not in any real sense. Nothing even happened to them, only *around* them—in their vicinity.

They bristle at Stacey, who admits, after hearing their complaints, that she has already arranged it, that a camera crew will attend their next meeting—not here but at Stacey's house—alongside the reporter. They'll sit in and record whatever content the group agrees to. The group responds that they'll agree to none of it, and Stacey says, Do what suits you, but I'm tired of my pain going ignored. Which makes them think Stacey will do it with or without them. They do not want her to speak for everyone, not to a camera crew or whoever may be watching when it airs.

Stacey has thickened up since she stopped running. She's told the group that running gave her routine and a way to control her body, and now that it's gone, she's tried all sorts of things that haven't worked. She doesn't like the low lighting and house music at spin classes. Yoga is an activity you can do lying down and therefore, she says, isn't sufficiently strenuous. She doesn't have the rhythm for Zumba or the flexibility for Pilates. She has admitted, in a hushed, secretive tone to each of the group members individually, that she worries her boyfriend will leave her. She thinks that her body and her grief are pushing him away. They picture her grief as a hand extending from her stomach—from the meat above her waistband, or her ass—to shove her boyfriend out of their shared bed and onto the carpet.

They do not know where her boyfriend is at this precise moment, other than *in the back*. He disappears behind a set of swinging doors periodically during each meeting, emerges holding packaged sports equipment: loose clubs and netted soccer balls, several pairs of women's crew socks in yellow. He doesn't speak to them, as if this will save him if it's ever found out that they meet after hours in his store—or rather, in the store he manages. Whenever he passes by the sneaker track, Stacey grows louder and bossier—performative, often talking out of turn. The group focuses on her boyfriend, rather than Stacey, during these outbursts. He refuses eye contact and retreats to the EMPLOYEES ONLY area again. He's in better shape than Stacey, and the group imagines that fitness might've been what brought them together in the first place. She might not be wrong about the growing distance between them, though the group is mostly concerned about where they'll hold meetings if the two of them break up.

They remain quiet after Stacey's latest acknowledgment of her pain and the space it takes up in the room. Always, as an unspoken rule, they wait longer to chime in after she speaks than they do with one another. They are clearing their throats, gearing toward the moment when someone will offer Stacey relief, when a buzzing starts up. *Zz zz zzz*—light but persistent, on repeat.

They look around where they're seated on the benches. They rise, begin pacing the track as the buzzing stretches on—fainter, then closer. They spread out, crouching and creeping to find the source.

Gotcha! says Jeremy, reaching between the stacks of clearance cleats and hoisting up a lit cell phone.

The rest of the group is miffed not to have found it first, though of course it doesn't matter at all. This is a collective of joggers, sure, but also—perhaps more importantly—of finders. Their competitive energy misfires with nowhere else to aim it.

CALL FROM MOM, says the screen, the phone vibrating still.

They shuffle back toward their seats at the track to wait it out, but incredibly, Jeremy slides his thumb to answer. The group shouts, No! No! They rip the phone from his grasp to hang it up. The screen flashes a four-second call. They glare at Jeremy, incredulous, and his eyes dart between their faces, trying to read his misstep, his jacket zipped up to the chin.

Right-o—I'll get this into good hands, he says. He takes off at a power walk toward fishing gear, where they spotted Stacey's boyfriend last. The group dismisses early in case the phone's location is being tracked.

Pete had been running against the advice of his doctor. He'd chosen the vacant lot, partially because it seemed like a cinematic place to train—with barrels to leap over and partially erected scaffolding that he could climb and lift himself through—and also because his father had been talking about it, had been out of work because of it. His father had theories as to why they'd stopped construction there—why they'd halted and left it fallow for a month now, the fenced entry strung through with a padlock. His father—a man who believed in conspiracies—heard that workers had tapped into something else entirely. A toxic vein or a burial ground, maybe oil or evidence of government testing. Pete wasn't sure if it applied here, but his father believed in aliens. Pete, meanwhile, suspected there was a simpler explanation: that someone in the chain of turning the lot from what it had been into what it would be next had run out of the money required to do so, and that his father had pissed someone off on his crew and hadn't been told about the next job.

Pete didn't want to fall out of shape and knew his body best when it was moving, knew himself best strong. His high school's practice field was locked on the weekends, the parks packed with kids and their soccer games, their screaming parents. The construction site and its busted fencing, its pits and piles of rubble—which Pete scaled and dodged when he trained there—made the lot an ideal location, both for Pete to run in and, as it turned out, in which to hide a body.

Pete had likely jumped over the body several times before discovering it. He'd grown tired from running in the heat, which bounced off the dust and rock and shivered up from the ground to meet him. He'd run in heat like this plenty of times at practice, but his doctor had said to take it easy for a while, which Pete hadn't. On this particular pass, he did not clear the lip of a rolled and rain-wet tarp, but instead caught it with his sneaker, causing its corner to unfurl and sending Pete sprawling into the dirt, scraping his shin against gravel as he fell. Pete cursed as he landed, and his earbuds ripped out, and it was in this position, curled on the ground in the complete silence of the lot without his noise to fill it, that Pete spotted what peeked from the lip of the unrolled tarp, which was a pair of feet: small, bluish; bruised and crossed at the ankles.

For what felt like a long while, Pete did not move at all. Blood wept from his shin, down through grit and into his sock, and he tried to imagine what lay before him as a hallucination, which the doctor had warned him could happen if he didn't rest or even, in some cases, if he did. He'd caught another boy's helmet against his in practice and had fallen out on the field, concussed. Pete was told that he had not lost consciousness, that he'd blinked up at his teammates from the grass, slurring when he answered the medic's questions, though he could not remember doing this or hitting the ground, or the initial pain that must've come from having his brain stung and rattled. He best recalled the too-loud crack that rang inside his helmet, the plastic between Pete and the other boy buckling on impact.

Pete found himself at Urgent Care with his father, with a doctor who said—gravely and, in Pete's opinion, unhelpfully—that there was evidence that permanent damage could occur from a single concussion. Pete's father had watched him closely since hearing this, trying to suss out if Pete was in any way changed.

Pete's coach said that doctors were paid to worry folks unnecessarily, that he himself had taken plenty of hits and stood up to ask for more. Just take it easy, Coach said, which Pete hadn't, because staying at home meant spending time with his out-of-work father, who didn't drink or yell like other fathers might in the same situation, but who instead cared too much for Pete, who changed Pete's bedroom lighting to accommodate bulbs that could be dimmed with the new switch he'd installed and who checked in incessantly. *You feeling dizzy, son? You'd tell me if you was?* Pete's mother had died young, and perhaps the suspicion that his father nursed closest was that life was slippery and always trying to leave them.

Once Pete had limped home from the lot, and his father asked what happened, meaning his leg, and Pete told him about the tarp, which he hadn't unrolled further; after they'd driven there and slipped through the gap in the fence to be sure that what Pete had found was real before calling anyone official; after the cops came and took their information and sent them away; and after his father had driven Pete home—for once quiet about the authorities' role in duping the masses—Pete hadn't thought about the body at all, really. He let it hover somewhere between hallucination and fact, let the details blur and merge so that he couldn't be sure of much.

His father read about the group on one of the online message boards he frequented for discussions on chemtrails or crop circles or raising teenage boys. He insisted that Pete go a few times, see if it helped. Now he drives Pete and waits through each meeting in the parking lot, listening to talk radio and dozing off in the driver's seat. Pete does not ask him to do this, is plenty capable of driving himself. But his father is trying. He is always trying.

Pete participates only enough in the meetings so as not to seem hostile. He listens to the group's stories queasily—all that blood and flesh and decay, the once-removed violence—though he tries not to let on that it bothers him. Squeamishness would not suit his image. If he thought about it, he might be thankful that his body—the body he found—had the decency not to bleed. He is the youngest of them, and he suspects it makes them pity him, when in fact they all seem so lonely to him, so vulnerable to a roomful of people they do not know. He finds their lives depressing, their chosen brand of athleticism depressing. He pictures them driving home after each meeting to heat up frozen dinners, feeling emptied out and hollow. He does not find a single one of them attractive, which perhaps explains his lack of imagination toward the lives they lead outside of the meetings.

Pete crosses his arms and disengages for most of the talk. He keeps an eye on Stacey's boyfriend whenever he crosses into view. Pete knows that the store has a guns and ammo section. Pete wonders if Stacey's boyfriend has the key, or if they even lock it up at all. Surely they do, though there's a certain carelessness to the idea of selling guns and golf tees and kids' shin guards all in the same place. He wonders if the rest of the group thinks about the guns and ammo section. He tries not to pick at the remains of the scab on his shin, though it itches. There's a hard spot just beside the bone that he thinks is a pebble lodged inside him, stuck underneath his skin gone shiny, trying to heal itself shut.

They've been burned by the media before, this group. Their distrust is natural, is how anyone would feel after what they've been through.

Imagine this: that the terror of what you've found isn't really yours, that there are others closer to the victim, the person killed—the person maimed or left untouched besides whatever ended them—and that in the moment of finding them, of rescuing them in a way, because even though you did not save them from death, at the very least they are now no longer missing, no longer kept alive but suffering in the minds of their mothers and lovers and the coworkers they shared a cubicle with, who glance over now and again at the still unoccupied desk and think, *If she's still alive, she's changed forever*, and there are more who know now besides the person gone—who, if the books are telling it correctly, thinks of themselves not as dead but as free, or cannot think of themselves as anything, or has joined the moss and dirt and fungal web of the ground that holds them now, which branches and feeds itself with them, keeping them alive in some way forever—and the person who did the killing and kept it to themselves, because it was you who took that secret away from them, on a jog along your favorite path while thinking of the stitch in your side or the heat in your ears or what you'd cook for dinner before you—in this moment that replays again and again or not at all—found yourself alone with a stranger who was no longer alive.

(How true could this be, though—that the group had given anyone relief? A missing girl is missed forever; a dead one, for a while.)

Who could the group place at the center of this—of their anger, their loss, their sudden aversion to meat drippings or a quick, clamped palm on their shoulder? Not the victims—the *real* victims, they call them, to make space for themselves. Their killers, sure, but they remain at large for the most part, and if the group thinks of them for too long, they are swallowed up by fear.

No, here is where the blame lands for most of them, where

they've decided to settle it: On the morning news after each incident, there'd been the footage of caution tape strung around tree trunks, poorly wrapped and already loose, lit up by a flicker of police lights, and investigators in unflattering khaki, hands at their bulky belt packs, or gloved and snapping photographs, bagging leaves and stones and other might-be evidence, before the screen flashed to a news anchor in a too-bright suit who said that new reports had surfaced of a suspected homicide in the valley, and each member of this ill-begotten group leaned close despite themselves to hear their part—

A local jogger found the body of—

And just as quickly as all that, their only role to play was over.

Joanna is almost her body exactly.

Like her body, Joanna is in her early thirties and white. She has two children and a husband, like her body. No job, besides homemaker—which is to say, many jobs. Joanna wonders if her body had hobbies like hers, if her body tried pottery. Or if her body took up portrait photography when the kids were babies and her mother wanted holiday cards, dressed the children as pumpkins or rabbits, or posed them like they were tumbling out of a neatly wrapped box. Joanna wonders if her body felt proud of the cards, or if she let them pile up well past the corresponding holiday, so that mailing them out would've caused more pity than joy.

Joanna's body went running in that crisp hour between daytime and unsafe—before husband home, before dinner. Her body was pushed from behind and damaged, like a moth rubbed clean of one wing's dust, left fluttering but already doomed. If Joanna's body was raped, it wasn't immediately apparent, because leggings had been pulled up, her face cleaned, hair retied. Pristine besides the obvious.

Joanna is able to recite these facts easily at group. The details themselves are not easy, but she can say them. She thinks the quick brutality, then repair, is important. She thinks it shows remorse. She told the police as much, and though her husband wants to know if she's okay, really, and though he has trained the children to be softer with her, to ask for less, and to never *ever* ask about *it* specifically, Joanna is actually fine with recollecting her body. She appreciates a lifetime of dread made concrete, the prickling at the nape of her neck rendered true.

Joanna's body is not her body because it's dead. Otherwise, it's her.

The group meets at Stacey's to shoot the TV spot. They file into her living room, which is surprisingly modest. They'd imagined her wealthy, but the furniture is unfussy and secondhand. The coffee table is scratched. The space is tidy, despite this.

Stacey has moved the table out of the dining room and set folding chairs in neat rows. She has arranged the group members by height—tallest in back—and has put scraps of paper with each of their names written out on the seat cushions. Sumarra's name graces a front-right chair, which is surprising because she's tall, but unsurprising because she's striking and also the group's only Black member, its only member of color at all. Pete's name is also up front because he's young, which suggests another kind of diversity. The group pulls faces at the notion of assigned seating, but they take their places. Stacey has made an elaborate cheese plate, and they all avoid the brie.

Mr. Harkin pivots in the front row to tell them that he and his wife are traveling to New York at the end of the month so that he can audition. There's a *Law & Order* episode set to film, based loosely around the bodies he found, the peculiar facets of the case: a car parked at a lovers' lane, an elderly couple seated inside with their hands clasped, serene but suffocated. Mr. Harkin was the vice principal of a private Catholic school, and some of his students parked at the lane on occasion, though he hoped more guiltily. He'd only noticed the car because he'd run by it parked there three mornings straight. The car was an older model, and when he jogged up to rap on its window, he imagined someone inside would need to roll it down with a lever. When he first relayed the story at group, he'd mimicked the motion by rolling his fist in a circle, as if none of them could fathom a car this ancient.

Mr. Harkin says his wife caught wind of the TV production, and though no one's asked him to audition specifically, he thinks he's a *shoo-in* for at least one part. He winks. They understand that this joke would've landed better on the sneaker track. They smile when he catches their eye but do not laugh. He's retired now, though he might've been soon anyway, at his age.

When it comes down to it, they let Stacey do the talking. It's a smaller crew than expected—only one cameraman and the reporter, who climbs out of the driver's side when the van pulls up and spits her gum into the grass by the curb. If Stacey sees this, she doesn't say anything, though she's at the window, watching. Once inside, the reporter looks around at the assembled group and deflates a bit, they think. They've dressed up without coordinating it, and they're uncomfortable out of their Lycra and elastic, without their reflective piping. Jeremy is wearing a turtleneck and brogues—his toes, for once, a mystery.

Stacey's boyfriend is not in the house, though there are men's shoes lined up in the cubbies by the door. The group suspects he's still after plausible deniability in case things come to a head, if their regular meeting place is somehow revealed.

Tell us what's brought you all together, says the reporter, somber now that things are set up and rolling. Her pantsuit is a muted sage.

I'd say, the worst run of our lives, says Stacey. She chuckles a bit, but stops and stays serious for the rest of the interview. Flippant could be the wrong look.

Did any of you know the victims?

No. I guess you couldn't say that. Only there at the end.

Could you describe to the viewers what it was like—finding them?

Different for each of us. Stacey looks around. Haunting, for sure.

Stacey gives broad, unspecific answers. She's speaking for the group, and they let her. She is asked how they're holding up, if they've found solace in finding one another. Stacey answers carefully. She is asked what they would say to each of the victims if they could.

We can't, she answers quickly, almost angrily. And then: I suppose we'd say, *Stay home. Stay safe and alive.* We'd say, *We're sorry.*

The reporter thanks them for sharing and wraps up the interview, speaking directly into the camera. The group looks into the camera, too. The reporter says, May this group of brave souls find their footing again soon. She doesn't blink until the recording light cuts off.

Okay, then, the reporter says to the group. Ready for part two?

It appears there has been some miscommunication. The reporter says she left a message on Stacey's voicemail, but Stacey says, no, she never got it. The reporter says it's the final shot, the end to their segment: the group all lined up together, ready to start fresh, taking one great stride in slow motion, hands joined on their journey toward whatever comes next—a running habit resumed, and the rest along with it. Normalcy, they imagine she means to imply. Routine. No more jumping at slammed doors, no distaste for dirt caught beneath their fingernails. Instead, moving on. Moving up. Graduations, promotions. Forward motion, however assumed. The scene of the crime just a running route once more—a park, a quarry, or their own quaint neighborhoods. There is trauma in the periphery, sure, but they've found some healing here. Together. The reporter says this last shot will give a sense of closure. She raises her manicured hands to place air quotes around the last word.

But they haven't brought a change of clothes, not one of them, and the group's not ready, anyway. Not willing to do a thing like that—potentially over and over, to get the shot just right—for an audience simply waiting to hear the weather forecast. They've been through enough already. Haven't they been through enough already?

The reporter is angry, despite her attempt to seem professional.

She says, once it's clear they won't cooperate, and not kindly, Best of luck with everything. She huffs out and leaves the cameraman to break down the lighting and sound equipment in a rush.

He's fumbling, pink and sweating though the room isn't hot. They want to help him but don't know how anything works or comes apart. Stacey disconnects her own mic and wraps the cord around it, stands to hand it over. The rest follow suit, though they never even used them—though they found the effect of wearing mics strangely silencing. The cameraman says they'll make it work as is, no worries. He seems like a nice man. He does not say when to watch for the segment.

Stacey sees him out, then comes back to the group and shrugs. As if to say, Sorry that things have gone this way, or that it might not air at all; sorry that she signed them up for this, and sorry for the rest of it: for their lives upturned, however briefly. For the time it might take to lace up trainers without thinking of ligature marks, or to consider solitude a gift, or to imagine their own bodies as swift and capable, rather than thin-skinned and full of fluid, prone to irrevocable harm.

They don't speak for a long while, or for a breath, and then they stand and drag their chairs to the perimeter, careful not to let them squeal across the tile. They help Stacey reset the room.

SENTRIES

MABEULAH ARRIVED FIRST, ALL BUSTLE and bags and hatboxes. She had come to see us plenty of times before, but never with quite so much stuff, and never with the intention to stay. My brothers and I were kept moving all day long, me slowed slightly by the hurt I was nursing. There'd been talk of the guest room—which we used mostly to store neglected toys and photo albums and things we'd meant to donate—being mine when I was old enough, so I could have space from the boys and all the gas leaving them and their tendency to shut me out of the room we shared. And now, with MaBeulah moving in, I'd have to wait, possibly forever. When I'd complained about this unfairness to my parents, Daddy asked if I preferred that we put MaBeulah on the porch instead, at her age, with nothing but a spring night to keep her warm and neighbors strolling by, wondering how he'd raised such selfish children as to put their great-aunt out. I said that I did not.

The first doll showed up not much later, maybe a week after MaBeulah had us waking up earlier and eating meals at set times—had my brothers and I answering the phone, *Harris residence, hello?*—even though she said she didn't want any fuss made, wouldn't have us changing routines on her account. I was sitting in Daddy's closet one evening while he was out fiddling in the shed, fixing this or that. Folks around town brought him busted items—farming equipment and lawn mowers and punched-through tires—and my father repaired what he could. The ghosts of what he could not save littered the shed. He worked on through the night, mosquitoes and my father crowded over the glow from a single bulb, tinkering the broken bits free.

I'd gone into Daddy's closet to take the shoehorns out of his dress shoes, to gather them up and shake them. I liked the sharp crack their heads made against the metal rods of their spines—like the maracas we played in music class, but meaner. I reveled in the racket and the audacity of making it. Noise was not well tolerated when Daddy was inside. If Daddy had found me, he'd have said, *Come outta there, Esther. You're too old for this.* And I'd have said, *How old's too old?* and he'd have said, *You.*

I swept my hand beneath the row of Daddy's work pants for more shoes and knocked something smaller aside. I pulled it out into the light where I could see better. A plastic doll lay in my palm, about the size of the green army men my brothers played war with, but black. A painted-on swatch of orange wrapped around its waist, but the doll's head and chest were bare. I traced its outline—bumps of breasts and behind, the tiny indent of its belly button, ridged feet—with a thrill running through my fingertip. What was it doing here? Was it Daddy's? The doll seemed too small a thing for him to fuss with. I swept my hand under the row again to check for more, but there were no clues, no more dolls in the closet's shadows. I raced out then, left the spines of Daddy's shoes on the floor in a heap.

My mother was in the living room smoking, wearing an apron and one rubber glove. I hadn't known she was home. She stayed late working at the salon most nights, came home to set something quick on the stove. While the rest of us ate, she'd settle into the chair by the TV and flip through the magazines that came to the house and piled up waiting for her. She'd chew the paint off her stick-on fingernails and turn the pages in quiet.

We reasoned that her job left her talked out—tired and absent, even when she was in the room. She rarely paid us mind as long as we kept clear. My mother seemed always dismayed to find children in her house, as if she was living at the mercy of a poor decision she'd made three times. My brothers and I did our best not to take this personally. Sometimes she'd look up from the page she was turning like she'd remembered something. The mess would come over her then, the tracks we'd left behind glimmering in the sudden glow of her attention. When Mama cleaned, it was all at once. She'd cancel her appointments and spend the whole next day at home, buffing the furniture slick and layering the air with a thick, lemon scent and remainder nicotine. Company brought the cleaning on stronger, and Mama had spent the last week poised to scrub.

"What is it?" she said now, settling back down to sit once she saw it was only me. I held the doll out to her now, told her where I'd found it. She took it, frowned. Mama ran her finger over its head, dimpled to mimic cropped hair. Some of the ash from her cigarette fell to the carpet, then blended right in. MaBeulah said smoking was a man's habit, but I thought it was a thing beautiful women did. I watched the smoke curl from Mama's cigarette, watched it separate and fade when it met the popcorn ceiling.

MaBeulah shuffled into the room in her housedress and slippers. She'd let her hair out of the curlers, had it combed and pressed into the shape it would hold all day. My brothers insisted that she wore a wig, that under all that hair, MaBeulah's scalp was bald and greasy. But whenever I looked for netting between those waxy curls, MaBeulah felt my eyes drift and scolded me before I could get a good look. When she saw the doll in Mama's hand now, she stopped and turned to leave the room again.

"Ma," Mama said, holding MaBeulah there, "do you know anything about this? What was it doing in Terry's closet?"

My brothers and I knew when we were caught, but I guess MaBeulah didn't, or didn't care when she was. She was slow to answer. "Don't worry about it, honey," MaBeulah said when she was ready, not even looking at Mama. And then, before Mama could respond, "Esther, let your mama get back to it. Lord knows this room could use some attention. Go and wash up. You look wild."

I looked quickly between the women and down at the doll before Mama tucked it into her apron pocket. I could see its shape, vaguely, against the fabric. MaBeulah left the room, left Mama's nostrils flared out and angry, and I followed before that mad could turn on me.

ON THE SPICE RACK; THE LINEN CLOSET

Before she came to stay, my brothers and I looked forward to MaBeulah's visits the same way we did a thunderstorm. She arrived at our doorstep on holidays, sometimes unannounced. For the three days or the week that she stayed, we watched our parents scramble, felt power shift in a way we did not quite understand, but cherished. They behaved around one another, spoke kindly. Mama beat rugs out over the clothesline, touched up her hair each time she passed a mirror or shined surface. Daddy got dressed for church and threatened to whup us if we got fresh about it, even though on the rare occasions we'd gone before, he never came with us. My brothers and I were given unfamiliar chores, were told off for the smallest mistakes. MaBeulah let our family scurry around her, stepped regally through the space we made.

On each visit, she toted exactly two suitcases—one brimming with hats and clothes and the things you'd expect, and the other full to bursting with food. My brothers and I would gather around, waiting for her to reveal the bounty she carried, the meals that would replace the instant dinners we were accustomed to. She shooed us away, barked at us to line up, to get useful. Miles organized us into a line, and we passed the parcels of food assembly-style into the kitchen. MaBeulah unpacked vegetables—both raw and canned, steeping in their own juices; big hunks of meat and gizzards and other parts we couldn't identify, all wrapped up tight, wearing plastic like skin; jars of grease and jellies; fresh, roadside eggs she'd picked up on the way to us; loaves of homemade bread. We'd never gone hungry in our house, but MaBeulah must've felt we lacked for something.

She always packed one extra ham, which was designated exclusively for my father's consumption. MaBeulah had raised Daddy and still spoiled him. Whenever our grandmother came to visit, our father was polite, quiet. Jumpy, even. It made us nervous, made it hard to know how to act. He was easy with MaBeulah, and so we could be too. We liked the title *great-aunt*, like she was better than the other, regular kind.

The combinations at work in her food enthralled us. She'd pour cans of Coke into a Crock-Pot to simmer with the roast. She brought hot pepper jelly for us to spoon onto crackers, made 7UP cake by pouring soda right into the batter. She believed in sugar and added it to everything—to deviled eggs and potato salad and even fruit. One Easter, MaBeulah brought fresh, cut strawberries, and when Mama popped the lid to find the slivers drenched in syrup, she snapped at MaBeulah that they were plenty sweet on their own.

"Just like you, honey," said MaBeulah. Our great-aunt winked at us, went back to the pot she was stirring, and we giggled without knowing what we were agreeing with. We stopped short when Mama turned to glare at us, choked down big gulps from our glasses of water that MaBeulah had sweetened with a pinch of sugar too.

UNDER BEDS; IN THE LAUNDRY BASKET

A home is only who's inside of it and what they do to keep each other. Before MaBeulah came to stay, ours had grown swollen with us. My brothers and I thought it small and flat and too tight to stretch in, too close to contain our parents and the hot, mad air between them. No space for all of that and us.

But with the dolls there, our house became vast. The carpet

was tufted, not with stains and vacuum burns, but with our family's history. The ceilings grew taller to make space for what lay beneath. We found new nooks and corners in our house, hideaways that were just the right size for a doll to find and settle into.

We pulled one doll from a blue glass vase we'd been forbidden to touch, found another in the soap dish, sitting plain as day. Eddie found a doll behind the encyclopedias that Daddy was always pushing us to read so that we might *educate* ourselves, so that we might *use* what God had provided to learn about His earth rather than just carrying on across it the way we did. We thought the lettered volume that hid the doll might be a clue, but after an exhaustive search through pages of cramped text and too few pictures, we turned up nothing.

We both looked for the dolls and didn't. They were identical, which made determining their exact number difficult. My brothers and I treated them like guests, tried to give them privacy as best we could manage, lest they grow tired of our pestering and stop appearing. Whenever we came across one, we'd startle, then remember ourselves. We'd turn away and whistle as if we hadn't seen anything at all. After a few hours or days had passed, we'd check on them again. Sometimes we found the doll, still waiting there. Other times, it was gone.

One night while we three were fighting sleep in our beds, we heard a shriek and came running. We found Mama in her bedroom, standing at the dresser with a doll in her outstretched palm, her hair dotted with pink and seafoam sponges. It must've been hidden among the curlers, and from the way she was glaring at Daddy in the mirror—at the spot that must have been his reflection behind her—she thought he was the one who had hidden it there.

There was often a fight in the room with the two of them, and because we couldn't see where it lay in wait, it was easy to trip over. The fight was feral. Usually, hollering about one thing set them off about everything. Or hissing at each other through their teeth about things we tried not to hear. But we'd seen it go differently, too, seen the two of them get soft and close with each other. The fight could go any kind of way. Mama closed the doll in her fist and Daddy shrugged, tried to look busy unlacing his shoes. My brothers and I backed out before this fight decided itself, took ourselves to bed. The lights in MaBeulah's room were out.

Miles felt that the dolls were in danger with Mama. She pocketed each one she found, and we suspected that the dolls did not come back from this. My brothers and I began a sort of relocation program for the dolls in our parents' room. We snuck in while they were gone and searched all the spots that the dolls liked in other rooms, poked through their drawers and pockets, which was not nosy because we were rescuing. If we found anything interesting—pill bottles or phone numbers jotted on paper corners or photographs of our parents looking younger and brighter beside people we didn't recognize, possibly before us—we made a note to return later, to check for the dolls again. We left everything as we'd found it but smuggled the dolls out to leave elsewhere in the house. For a time, we were hiding the dolls for one another to find, though that was never our intention.

We understood that the dolls' presence and MaBeulah's were linked, that there was a connection between her stay with us and theirs. MaBeulah moved around the house—cleaning and cooking and watching the news at a too-loud volume—and we followed behind her, investigating. We tried to imagine how she could be managing it—how she was climbing stools and reaching beneath furniture to deposit dolls. We took in her swollen knees and ankles streaked purple with veins. We watched her hands and pockets, the sharp way she eyed a stubborn piece of grit in a dirty pot. We felt the way she drove us out of the room when she caught us spying, how she made us brush our teeth and finish homework without speaking. We figured the dolls were similarly mindful.

Sometimes, if I came across one when I was alone, I'd pocket it and keep the discovery to myself. In this way, I built up a small collection. I'd wait until MaBeulah was sleeping, then tiptoe in and leave two or three on her dresser. I was asking her a question, maybe, or else I just liked the sight of them lined up together, the idea of MaBeulah waking up to see them looking over her. In the morning, I'd cut back in to find them gone, and she'd treat me a little sweeter at breakfast.

"Esther," she might say, "you'd better eat up and get to that bus before it leaves you." And then, "Oh, lord. Sit still a minute. What've you done with your hair?"

I'd taken to fixing it myself and thought it looked fine, but the back was done blind. MaBeulah shuffled over and yanked one crooked braid loose, and while she was plaiting it back, I closed my eyes, felt her hands in my hair, rubbing through my scalp. She drew the line of my part with a fingernail, let it whisper down my spine and through the rest of me before she pushed me out the door again.

ON A PANTRY SHELF; OUR BACKPACKS

Two summers before she lived with us, MaBeulah unveiled her newest culinary undertaking. She hefted two large jars from the folds of her suitcase. Inside, large and grubby somethings bobbed in colored brine. My brothers and I spun the jars in the kitchen. The liquid in one was a dark, thin red; the other was the bruise-color of a rain cloud.

"Kool-Aid pickles!" MaBeulah said, coming in behind us.

My brothers and I were ecstatic. The prospect of two of our favorite things, mashed up in such an unexpected union, felt to our young souls like the world opening up to us, like the universe showing its hand. MaBeulah bade us wash up before we could try them, and when we came back to our plates, she had cut the spears in half and given us both flavors to try. We gazed at the Seussian meal before us—the pickles stained with dye, their fleshy insides and seeds gone pink from black cherry flavoring, gone lavender from grape. The puddles beneath them combined to a blush in the middle of the plate. Still grinning, we each took a massive first bite.

It's hard to say what happened for the boys, but my mouth was thrown into turmoil. MaBeulah had poured the dill brine out of the jars and filled them instead with the sickly sweet punch of imitation fruit juice. The result was all syrup and vinegar, the flavors charging up against one another. I rolled the pickle across my tongue to find the parts that might have harmonized, but the clash was the point. There was no part untouched. I gulped it down, tried to keep my face straight since MaBeulah was watching us. I looked at my brothers and the wetness in their wide eyes and knew the game was up. We looked down at our remaining pickles, looked up at our expectant great-aunt.

"Well, fine," MaBeulah said. "I hate it for y'all." She snatched up the jars and replaced the lids, huffed back over to the sink and turned her back to us.

She did not take our plates. We glanced at one another and steeled ourselves, ate up the remaining halves, and grimaced as much as we needed to while she couldn't see us. Miles and Eddie and I spent the rest of that weekend's visit trying to make it up to MaBeulah, eating her homemade cracklins and liver pudding with gusto. She left the jars of pickles on the counter, and we would sneak one out at a time to feed to the strays behind the house. We wanted her to see them disappearing, but even the dogs thought about letting them alone.

BEHIND CURTAINS; IN THE COOKIE TIN

She meant to civilize us. MaBeulah taught us to place our napkins in our laps and to use them, rather than the wrists and sleeves we had gotten away with before. She was vigilant about socks, said the cold would seep into our bones without them. When we slid them over our calloused feet, MaBeulah caught sight of the cracked skin at the backs of our heels and lost her mind all over again. Under her watch, we rubbed ourselves down with enough lotion to make us dread sweating.

MaBeulah told Daddy he'd raised us like hooligans. *Hooligans,* we shouted at one another, jumping from behind doors and curtains. *Hooligans!* It was the funniest word we'd ever heard. We thought she'd made it up especially for us.

If we sensed our parents coming apart, it was a drawn-out premonition. They hid their fighting from MaBeulah so that if we children stayed close, we could pretend that the rooms we entered were not tensed up and mad. A broken plate on the kitchen floor was simply swept away. Daddy came home one evening, swaying and smoke-thick in the living room. He did not usually drink but nursed a soft spot for the combination of grapefruit juice and shine. Two sets of shaming eyes sent him straight to bed that night, the women united for once.

MaBeulah kept us in line, and for the most part, our family took to it. But my brothers and I fought MaBeulah on some things. She wouldn't let us drain the bathwater between our hurried baths—said that we had come from the same water, wouldn't hear whining about it now. As the oldest and biggest, Miles got the first bath, got piping hot water and the feeling of leaving clean. Eddie and I got what remained, and whoever went last left the bath wearing the other two. MaBeulah caught Eddie and me wrestling with the bathroom door one night, his fingers wrapped around the edge I was trying to pull shut, both of us leaning in opposite directions and squinting at what would happen when one of us won—smashed fingernails, maybe bones crushed flat. When MaBeulah found us there with the door wavering between us, we told her we'd rather die than get in that water last.

"That just might happen, sooner than you think if y'all keep tryin' me," she said. "Get in and wash up before I throw you in there together." We believed her always. MaBeulah had follow-through and little patience for regret. She taught Daddy what he knew about whuppings, and my brothers and I feared the strength of it from the source. I let Eddie go first and found a doll caught in the drain once I'd let the bathwater out.

Mama spent more time at the salon, or somewhere else, and the nights when she came home felt special. She might call me into her bedroom to ask about my math test or the songs I'd memorized in choir. It seemed that time away from us had renewed her interest, if only slightly. Mama's attention trailed off toward the end, same as always, but I felt grateful to her for asking, made sure her stacks of *Jet* and *People* stayed neat on the coffee table. I might've blamed MaBeulah for Mama gone, but perhaps it was a gentler choreography: one mother for another, the house warm and bright enough to cover the difference.

Daddy remembered us in spurts. He took time to teach us skills he thought important, though I could discern no clear link between them. We learned to spin quarters, to whistle, to thump one another on hollow skin so that there was depth to the sound that rose up afterward. One night, when Mama had stayed gone a whole week and MaBeulah was in bed, Daddy gathered the boys and me at the dinner table. He held each of us in his gaze until we went quiet. It looked like he had something to say.

Instead, Daddy began to shift his scalp, just barely at first. His hairline wavered, wrinkled back and forth. It picked up speed, so that his forehead seemed loose over his skull. Daddy turned to the side then, so we could see the reason, could see his ears dancing loose from the rest of him.

"You just have to feel it," Daddy said, laying his ears still. "Find the muscle." He pushed his chair out and went to bed.

My brothers and I tried to mimic the motion. Miles was quick with everything but schoolwork and picked it up immediately, even managed to vary the speed of his wiggle. Eddie's ears moved, too, but barely. I found that I could only raise my eyebrows. I brought my hands up to pull my ears back over and over, told my skin to remember the feeling. I tied my hair up in case it helped.

"Show me where the muscle is," I demanded of my brothers when it didn't.

Miles smiled at me, his arching forehead making the grin a leer. "Maybe you don't have it," he said. "Maybe *girls* don't." He and Eddie laughed, stood up to leave me there. They could be cruel, and crueler together because I was alone. I lost the motion of their ears in the dark.

Later, I lay in bed prodding the knobs of my skull with my fingertips, trying to sense the nerve for each place I touched. I tugged on my earlobes, let my hair back down. MaBeulah wheezed in the room next door, and I wondered if she couldn't do it either, if she would try if I asked her to. When I finally fell asleep, it was with a headache thumping beneath my baby curls, with my ears still and stubborn as always.

IN SOCK DRAWERS; OUR JACKET POCKETS

I was standing at the bathroom mirror after school one day, frowning at my reflection and pressing my shirt flat at the chest with my palms, when Miles caught me at it. He threw the door open without knocking, and we froze, both of us waiting.

It was a time of preoccupation with my burgeoning body, with what was coming over me and out. The skin across my chest—once smooth and even like my brothers'—had gone tight and hot and painful. Tendons from my spine or somewhere else at the back of me had crept forward and knotted up just underneath my nipples. I was glad that breasts were coming, excited for what they might mean for whom I would become. But the ache of them was something I had not been prepared for. They hurt worst when I touched them, which I did constantly.

I like to believe that my brother weighed compassion, finding me there. That Miles considered closing the door and leaving me be. What he did instead was laugh—a great, booming laugh that screwed up his whole face, made him ugly at my expense. He pointed at me, still hooting.

"Whaddya got there, Esther?"

And then, "You know they'll stay put on their own, don't you? Even without you holding 'em."

He was going with a girl at school who wore frayed skirts and strawberry body spray and never came around the house with him. I imagined that he thought himself grown, though it didn't make him any kinder. He called for Eddie, and I shoved past. I ran to the shelter of MaBeulah's empty room, slammed the door behind me.

"Esther Ann," she warned from the living room. MaBeulah did not suffer slammed doors or tears, especially from me. She tromped down the hallway, set Mama's wedding china to rattling in its cabinet. She found me hiccuping on the bed, tears puddling in the quilted grooves, pitiful. It was unfair, too much. I told her what happened, felt the pressure of the bed on my chest, and sobbed anew.

"All right, now," she said, rubbing my back. "Hush. We been through worse than this." She asked what Miles knew about anything, asked if I was going to let him upset me like this. I didn't answer, kept carrying on into her bedsheets.

"Do you know the kind of women we come from?" MaBeulah asked. She pulled a doll from her dress pocket. I was shocked to see it there in her palm, though I'd known it was her, must've known it was her. When our garbage disposal seized up the week before, Daddy had found a mangled doll caught in the blades. He'd fished it out and carried it to MaBeulah's room, had closed the door behind him. He might've told her to quit, though I couldn't imagine anyone telling MaBeulah off. The dolls had thinned out since. Part of me was disappointed at the reveal now, at the end to the mystery, but I didn't say so.

MaBeulah said we came from strength. "From *these* women," she said, doll in hand. "Ain't no shame in them, baby, and none in us. Women who brought up their children, they husbands too. Women who came through all that to raise up and ululate anyway."

You-yu-late. I sat up, curled the word around my tongue the way she said it to find its meaning. I shrugged at her.

MaBeulah smiled and leaned back. All at once, a great, rolling yelp leaped from her open mouth, lashed at the quiet around us. The sound bounded toward the ceiling, filled up the whole room. It was loud, wavered like something hurt or angry, perhaps most surprising because it came from her, had been pent up inside MaBeulah. Her tongue smacked the roof of her mouth over and over, faster than I knew it could move—the sound alive and pitching—and my heartbeat raced alongside it.

Once Miles and Eddie reached the doorway, MaBeulah closed her mouth. The sound whipped shut, and MaBeulah stood to leave like she had given me an answer. My brothers' wide eyes—at the sound itself, at the tattling that might've brought it on and what was coming to them for it—bore into me before the door closed, before I was alone with the rest of that call still burrowed in the walls. MaBeulah left a doll on the bed beside me. I didn't take it, though she must've meant it was mine.

IN THE TOILET TANK; THE ICE MAKER

MaBeulah left us when the heat did. We woke one winter night to the smell of smoke and found MaBeulah at the living room furnace, setting the house on fire. Daddy charged in last, bare-chested and still blinking the sleep from his eyes. Once he understood the room, he yelled for me to get MaBeulah, told the boys to run for water.

The smoke or the rest of it made my eyes stream, but I blinked through, tried to push MaBeulah away from what she'd started. She stared at the flames and the black stain spreading before them, didn't seem to notice me or my prodding at all. I had never laid hands on her that way, but I pushed until she budged, moved, until we were outside and past the porch and in the front lawn. We sat in the grass and watched smoke crawl from the front window, our bare feet pale in the dawning light. MaBeulah laid my head in her lap like I was the only one scared.

She told us she'd gotten cold. After Daddy and Miles and Eddie had tamed the fire without much damage, and a group from the church had been in—after they'd cleaned most of the soot from the ceiling and patched what needed it, and we'd eaten and settled down—MaBeulah said the cold had crept into her bed and under her sheets. She said it shook her awake, said she stoked the fire to keep the cold from reaching us.

But why hadn't she used the wood? Daddy asked. How had it gotten away from her?

MaBeulah didn't know.

She was softer with us after. The fire had burned some trust out of the house, on our end or hers. She spent more time in her room, slept in late. When she did come out, she wore the bonnet she slept in, didn't bother with the curls at all. MaBeulah phrased her orders like requests, took longer to settle on our names. Her temper dulled to something we didn't recognize. I carried bowls of soup to her bedroom, like she was sick, and MaBeulah thanked me before sending me back, reminding me gently to dilute the pot with water.

My brothers and I stopped waiting for someone to tell us to clean up, to take care of ourselves. This happened nearly instantly, as if we'd delayed growing older for the sake of the adults around us so that they might find their shape in our care, instead of the other way around. Daddy, in his shed more than ever. Mama least of all. She'd come home late that afternoon, after we'd cleaned up. The furniture was still in the yard, airing out, and Mama picked through it, stepped into the bare living room, quiet. She seemed embarrassed by the not-being-there or by the coming-back, maybe, but the truth was we hadn't looked for her. She was not the worst part, or really any part at all.

That night, in the lawn, with the fire inside, I'd thought of the dolls burning up. Those dolls in their hidden places—the backs of cabinets, between stacks of newspapers, crammed beneath a mattress. Could've sworn I heard their ululation—a warning, a calling out. Even after they were fine, after Daddy asked MaBeulah if she didn't want to stay with our aunt for a while—didn't she want some rest?—and after she went, after I got my own room and the house was all closed doors and MaBeulah's boxes stuffed into corners, I thought of the dolls lying cold and lonely because we hadn't found them. There, still. A house gone quiet, filled up with something we wouldn't look for, because finding it made it gone.

CERTAIN TRUTHS
AND MIRACLES

AT FIRST, RAFA THINKS THE altered sea is a trick of the home brew he has consumed in abundance. His vision is bleary—the edges dazed—and surely this is to blame for the scene before him. Past the breaking waves, the water is nearly calm, and it holds the sky's reflection: the wide, flat black of night; the moon half-full and glaring. But the stars on the water's surface are wrong.

They are not the dimmed hue of faraway starlight. These stars are turquoise—almost the color of the water in daytime—and caught in glimmering clusters. They swarm through the crests of waves, dim when they meet the shoreline. Rafa blinks to clear his eyes, but the sea's stars remain—perhaps the mirror image of a brand-new sky. Rafa needs some things to remain constant.

He looks up, and the motion sends him reeling. When his vision clears, he sees that the sky above is as he has always known it, the stars there still and fixed. Those below, then, are something else. Rafa exhales and vomits a rush of sour liquor into the sand. He slides back into his sandals and runs for the watchman's hut, sure that light caught beneath the brim of the sea is a sign meant for more than just him.

*

Dinoflagellata translates roughly to *whirling scourge.* The plankton responsible for a sparkling sea travel in dizzy patterns, eddied by marine currents. They appear nocturnally as quick spasms of light against the darkened ocean, their flash triggered by disturbance. They are most evident to us at shorelines, where wavebreak and thinning tides cause a blue-green glow, the result of countless organisms flickering—in alarm, defense, or warning—all at once.

*

Rafa's knocking rouses only the watchman's mother at first. She is cross but accustomed to covering for the shortcomings of her son, who dozes undisturbed by the door. She follows Rafa, trudges to the water to verify his words, tainted as they are with stale drink. Once she has seen the floating stars for herself, she tells Rafa to call for the others.

The woman stands gazing for a while after he leaves. A thing she's known all her life is new again. When she returns home, she'll begin to map it. She plans to stitch a tapestry, a quilt that will cover the floor, the yard, the whole island pressed flat if it must. But she will find her supplies inadequate—her thread and beads too dull and lifeless. She'll spend days bent down at the shoreline, collecting shards of glass and shells, loose scales. And even then, when she cannot get the stars quite right, she'll scratch into dark blue fabric with her fingernails, careful not to puncture it. She'll step into open air and raise the worn swatches above her. She'll stretch them to let the moonlight through. This will be the best likeness to the sea spread before her now, newly thin and pocked with light.

✦

The watchman's hut is one of a cluster. The island's dwellings are built tight and close to save space at the edges, and each hut leaves its door open to the next. Neighbors wander freely over all the island but one corner, which is home only to throngs of mosquitoes and the things that can tolerate them. The sand is plush and sticky, packed down in some places like sugar. The island itself is one of many, a collection strewn through the ocean like handfuls of grit dropped from the sky.

Once, a country that bordered the same ocean tried to lay claim to the island. Droves of men pulled to shore with weapons and flags and bravado, intent upon planting all of it there in the sand. The islanders met their invaders at the beach. They took them to the island's center, where the islanders danced and clapped. They fed the strangers and drank with them into the night. When the soldiers were merry and weighed down with shelled meat, the island's women tugged them into their hammocks.

The invaders slept, sated with their new bounty. They woke or did not wake to their own swords creasing the skin at their throats. That morning, the islanders carried the bodies far into the sea and dropped them there for the sharks. They washed the blood from their boats and homes, buried any stained sand deep. The houses smelled of liquor and metal for a time, and then of smoke and sea again. This happened exactly once.

*

They celebrate the sea stars. For a week, the islanders reverse the order of their days, stay up late to watch the sea at night. They press their feet into the shoreline and then step back to find their steps illuminated. The glow fades and they repeat, the miracle both inevitable and surprising each time. They bring their children to the shore—their lovers, too. They watch the water pooled in their palms sparkle and then fade to clear as it seeps through.

Rafa stands apart, wary as he often is of the islanders gathered in crowds—their steep belonging to one another. There is the old woman for whom he peels coconuts, her fingers gone too stiff to cleave meat from rind. There, the group of boys he'll join for games of soccer—the quick-footed one at the group's center, their plump keeper leaning in from the edge. Rafa knows the island's drunks by name, is testing out his place among them, though they offer a fight as often as a kind word or cool glass. They, too, stand in witness, swaying at the fringe. None of the islanders are immune to wonder, not even Rafa. And besides, the stars are his—Rafa's discovery first, despite what the watchman boasts. Rafa feels responsible for their reception now, for the spectacle they bring.

One child gathers the water in his cheeks, then turns to show those standing at the beach his glimmering mouth. The crowd applauds. They cheer him on. The child swallows a mouthful and repeats, each time tilting his head back so that his parents may gasp at the stars he has captured across his tongue. In time, they remember themselves, remember the sea and the danger of taking in too much of it. They pull their boy farther back onto shore. The boy digs into sand, perhaps trying to determine the shape of light. He stamps the stars out by burying them, and then unearths them again.

Days later, his parents will insist that he is glowing—a subtle and healthy daytime hue. By night, they say, the child is a shimmering conduit of the sea's bright light. It hardly lets them sleep.

Beni! Our Benito, they say, he wears the stars inside him!

Their neighbors nod and agree, pinch at the boy's cheeks and soft spots. More visitors stop by each evening to see him, to touch the boy's gleaming skin. Young Beni enjoys the attention, understands little. He sleeps deeply, and his parents divine the stars behind his features with their fingertips.

✦

The shimmering effect of a plankton-thick basin results from a chemical reaction, similar and yet distinct in function from a firefly's glow. While the insects flicker to attract mates, the plankton do so as a defensive strategy. At the slightest hint of movement, they set their surroundings alight, startling predators either with the flash or with the threat of what else it may lure. Plenty of aquatic life relies upon darkness for survival. Some of the plankton are predatory themselves, or parasitic, though most draw their energy from light.

*

There is a story of beginnings that the islanders tell and retell. They say that Sun came first into the sky. He was bold and bright, and his light filled up the world beneath him. After the plants and animals, Sun sent his rays to the island to make people. The islanders were born of his warmth, and Sun watched them build and grow and love. When Sun pressed close, their skin browned at the places he touched. Sun marked the people and the island each day, and they turned their faces skyward toward him in thanks.

Moon was lonely. She watched from a distance and came late into the sky to find only animals and deceit sneaking across the island's surface in her glow. When she tried to send light to the surface, she found it did not reach. She wavered in strength and size each night, and at most, all she could create were stars. She filled the sky with them, but the stars were cold and far from those below. Some evenings, the people wove stories from what Moon made in the sky—her constellations. But their traces faded in the daytime, outshone by Sun's hot light.

Not out of jealousy or anger but of her poor, broken heart, Moon wept. Her tears fell to the earth and puddled there each night, left pools that brimmed and sloshed. The people grew afraid. By day, they asked Sun to correct the mess that Moon was making, and he did as best he could, drawing the water up before he left the sky.

Moon felt unwanted and unloved. She decided to leave the sky.

One final tear of farewell slipped down the crags of her face and landed on the island as she turned away for the last time. But she heard a strange cry, an echo of her own mourning coming from below. She looked back to find a child taking shape in the puddle of her tear—a white and gleaming infant; bright skin, pale eyes. The child's wailing woke a couple, who came out into the night. They saw the full, bright Moon, and the calm rhythm of the tides and understood. They collected the child and brought her inside to raise as their own. By day, they shielded the child from Sun, kept her safe from his scorching rays. And on nights when Moon looked her best—when she was full and shining—they sent the child out to gaze at her mother.

From then on, pale babies were born to browned parents, a ripple of Moon's first gift. The Sun and Moon Children were mixed among the islanders, and on nights when Moon was full, her children stepped out to bask in the glow that made them.

⁂

Here are the things that Rafa cherishes most: a glossy, creased image of an orange convertible, cut from an advertisement; a handkerchief he believes to be his mother's; a large, glass bowl filched from an abandoned hut, one side of which is flawed and whorled like a soap bubble; a tattered and weather-worn stack of *National Geographics*—remnants of some outsider's mission to bring the island a library—in which Rafa reads about places he'll never visit and phenomena he may never witness; a shell that makes a hollow and satisfying whistle each time the wind blows through it; the dried umbilical cord of a brother Rafa never met; a jagged knife, used to pry meat from mollusks and to clean beneath fingernails; a jersey, emblazoned with the name of his favorite striker; three perfect silver dollars and a four-limbed starfish the color of rust and gums; the vein inside the elbow of his left arm, which fades when he presses it and then reappears to snake back toward his heart.

*

The people of the island believe in certain truths and miracles. They respect heat and salinity, and value the combination of both. Tears, sweat, urine, semen—each confirms their place at sea. They laugh often, note marriage and divorce by a redistribution of hammocks. The men cheer at thunder and storm clouds, daring them both to come closer. At birth, their babies' feet are rinsed clean and then pressed into sand to acquaint them with the ancestors ground down below.

Day after day, the granddaughter of one of the elders records history from beneath them, the stories pushed up between grains of sand. The elder lies with his ear pressed to the ground, translates what he hears to the girl. She gathers these whisperings of the past, and in this way, the people know what they have been. By day, the elder's granddaughter wears her skin smeared with grit and oils to protect her light complexion. Her pale hair peeks from beneath a cap, and the set of her head—bent down to hear her grandfather—is stern and sure.

She stands beneath a sunshade, stock-still for hours. Rafa has seen it for himself more than once. Even when it seems her grandfather may be sleeping, lying there against the sand, she waits. Only twice has she caught Rafa watching, looking up to meet his eye. On these occasions, she has seemed unsurprised to find him there, lurking in shadow. Her expression does not change. She holds him like that for the space of several breaths, then looks down to the elder again. Each time, Rafa stalks home and chides himself to stay away.

When the sea stars appear, the islanders ask the elder's granddaughter if they have ever come before. But this is not how the histories work, she says. The island does not answer; she does not ask. Their charge is only to listen, each day turning more present to past to feed the steady pace of time.

✳

The plankton are a hardy and persistent force, among the oldest of the earth's forms of life. There is much to be learned about their patterns and behaviors, more species yet to be discovered. They are most prevalent in marine environments, though some live in freshwater and brackish bodies between the two. In the coldest parts of the world, they gleam through shelves of sea ice. Some colonies can be seen from the height of space, swaths of the once-dark ocean gone milky with living light.

✳

They say Rafa's father was an unmoored fisherman, that Rafa was made in a single, desperate night. They say that Rafa was not the result of love, but of opportunity.

Rafa's mother, even after her son was born, wore a thick and weighing sadness. The other islanders avoided it—avoided her—

fearful that such sorrow might be catching. As a child, Rafa fetched the things his mother needed and then returned to find her—still home, still sleeping—just as he'd left her. He would curl into her again. They had routine, and each other.

But just as any mother might, Rafa's kept secrets from her son. Soon, she was expanding. She did not want another child, but Rafa did, desperately. On some nights, he spoon-fed his mother and imagined his sibling growing with each bite. Now, an earlobe. Now, fingernails and a nose like his.

When the labor pains came, the women did, too. Neighbors entered the hut and cooled his mother's forehead, pushed Rafa out to make room. When the delivery turned, they called him back to say goodbye. A family, almost three, now Rafa alone.

After, the women were left to care for him. They kept Rafa fed and clean, cycled him among their houses and children. But they found the boy serious, too grown for his age. He brought them gifts and took on chores while the other children played. Perhaps the mothers felt guilty, or unnerved. Perhaps they were only tired or had a finite amount of love to give and even less to spare. There were other things that required their attention, other gaps on the island that needed filling. They nursed a space between themselves and the boy until Rafa pulled away, too. In time, he learned to pretend that solitude was a choice.

*

The islanders depend almost entirely on water. They eat from the water, fill their bellies with the creatures that live in its depths. The tide brings crabs and fish, takes away the waste that they become.

It brings boats and neighbors and stray tourists and their stores of fresh water, of supplies and misguided charity. What they cannot use of rainfall is converted back to sea.

The water's rush is the background refrain of entire lives spent. A few have tried to leave it—moved somewhere inland where the sound of washing waves is too far away to hear. If their aunts and childhood friends can be believed, they've emptied out without it—their veins gone brittle and dry.

The water is the islanders' constant—both their center and their perimeter. It is largely predictable. They feed the sea their dead.

*

Every night since the sea stars, Rafa has walked the shoreline. He goes out after the others have yawned through their awe and retired for home. On one of these walks, he sees the elder's granddaughter in the water. He steps back, away from the shore. She is alone. The water climbs and recedes from the backs of her thighs, and the rings where she meets the sea sparkle with light. Her fingertips glint where they break the surface. She is nude and bright against the moonlight, or for it, her back turned to the trees that hide Rafa.

He watches her dip beneath the water's surface in one smooth motion. Almost as soon as she's gone under, Rafa loses the pocket of waves that hold her. She stays under for a long time, so long that Rafa begins to tense toward her rescue. Finally, she breaks the surface and stands. She is glowing with light and more light, moon and stars above her and upon her, coursing down her brilliant frame. A knot crawls up Rafa's throat—a caught urge to cry out. He could join her. One singularity draws another, and perhaps she could be his—the stars, theirs together.

Instead, Rafa races home. He is rushing, hears rushing in his ears. He takes the glass bowl from his room and cradles it in his arms, runs back to the beach. The elder's granddaughter is gone, and Rafa panics for a moment, thinking that she might have slipped beneath the water's surface for good. He waits for her to rise, or for the stars to cluster up beneath the waves to reveal her. He waits longer than a breath can hold, then steps out of shadow. He spots her footsteps leading away from the water, the puddles there bright only with moonlight.

Rafa treads into the shallows and dips the glass into the water. He avoids collecting sand. The stars bead up around his hands and legs, around the globe of the bowl before they slip in. He captures them, lifts the bowl out to see the bits magnified by the whorl.

Rafa walks inland, careful not to let any water spill. The bowl lights his chest, likely lights his face from below. As he traces her path back to the elder's hut, Rafa sees the glow of firelight in the distance—someone else awake. He considers how strange it is to be tucked so close to a heatless light—the glass in his hands the same temperature as the night and the cold, dark sea. The contents slosh and glimmer with each of Rafa's steps.

The elder's hut is dark and quiet, and Rafa places the bowl before its threshold. He takes several steps away and turns back to see it: the doorway illuminated by the bowl's roiling light. He means the stars as a gift, a wish. Perhaps, as an apology. If the elder's granddaughter is awake to receive it, she does not emerge, for which Rafa is grateful. He hopes she'll find it in the nighttime, when the stars are at their surest.

✦

The watchman's mother sees the danger coming. Just before Rafa leaves his token at the island's center, she startles in her hut at the island's edge. In the midst of stitching the color of sandshore against a waning curl of moon into her quilt, a feeling comes over the woman. She stops. She pulls away from the fabric and stands. Fate has taken a tone she cannot abide.

She acts quickly, automatically. She gathers the unused shards of fish bones and glass and sea-bleached wood, carries the debris outside. She makes a pile in the sand. She cuts her fingernails short and tosses the clippings into the pile. The woman builds a fire in the clearing beside the house. With her back turned to the water, she first tears the slivers of things loose from her tapestried sea. She feeds the fire the bones and bits, and once it's roaring, she tears the quilt itself apart and tosses the pieces in. They char and glitter and pop in the heat.

How long does it take to burn a doomed sea? She waits until the fire turns to coals. While the cinders dim, she digs a hole in the open sand. She buries the ashes of the future she has sewn, smooths the spot down flat.

The watchman's mother returns to her hut. Her son is sleeping, and she pauses in the doorway to watch his face slacken and twitch. She has kept him too close, she knows. She has coddled him, and his shortcomings are the result of her stern devotion. She has left him ill-equipped to cope with what's to come. But this is a mother's job and all she knows to do: to keep what's dearest safe; to keep it tender; at all costs, to keep it whole.

*

Most dinoflagellates are born of fission: a single-celled organism splits to two, then four. One cell becomes a hundred within weeks. With favorable environmental conditions, the cycle goes unchecked. Whole bodies of water teem with one thing halved into thousands and more. Such a bloom depletes resources, the plankton multiplying all the while. They crowd the surface—one flickering mass. A sea poisoned with light.

*

In a day, young Beni is warm with fever, which his parents take as a sign of impending transformation. He is pale in daylight, brilliant by night. They can no longer pick out each separate speck of light beneath his skin, and they assume that the bits have fused with his blood and organs. They feed Beni nocturnally and take him back to the sea whenever he asks, which is often.

Beni falls quiet—in contemplation, they think. His parents sleep through one night's vigil and, in the morning, find him cold. They tell no one, cover him with blankets. They coo and scold him as they always have. When night falls and he does not stir—when the light in his eyes is glassy and flat—their wailing brings the island running.

The body is incandescent. His parents shield their eyes with their fingers. They grasp at each other, unfamiliar with their shape without the child between them. The neighbors want to turn away in sympathy, but instead, they stare—squint—at the glowing boy gone still.

The next evening when the child's parents have succumbed to a deep and grieving sleep, a group of women untangle the child from his parents' clutches. They stand back from the body and let their sons carry it away. They tell the young men to be careful, to be quick. They tell them to give the boy back to the sea. Don't brush his skin, the mothers say, though the warning is likely too late. How many of them have already touched the boy turned bright? How many of them have cupped the stars?

Their sons carry Beni to the beach and dig into the shoreline. If they are frightened of the specks of light puddling in the grave, they do not say so. With each shovelful of sand over him, the child dims. The young men mark the spot with a large stone when it's done, but the grave is unmistakable from a distance—a faintly glowing mound in the shoreline. They shiver and trudge home. They will try again in daytime. Perhaps they will carry him out to sea.

By morning, the marker is gone, and the location of the boy's body is approximate and wearying.

※

Here is Rafa, just before the stars:

He is approaching manhood, toeing its edge, but he is still, in most of the ways that matter, a boy. It is much too late to be walking the shoreline. Rafa knows that the creatures beneath the surface are feeding, and that he could become a meal for the largest of them. And yet, Rafa is considering a swim.

He has lived by the sea his whole life. He can entice the largest crabs, knows when a conch is ready. His hair and skin are permanently brined. Rafa feels the pull of tide even when he is dry, judges the strength of an approaching storm by the height of the hairs on his arms. He knows how much of the sharp, fermented home brew is too much to warrant swimming and he has ingested that amount and more.

The water beckons, each curling wave a summons before it slaps back down. Rafa knows that no one drowns on an island, but he thinks that some must try. And then, suddenly, the water is spotted with light—with a hundred shimmering bits, like beacons of something more.

✦

The stars bring trouble, and then they take. The islanders are afraid of what the stars will take next. What they will take last.

They protect their small stores of groundwater. They quarantine saved rain, then bring it into the night to inspect for errant light. The islanders trust the night to show them the stars but are afraid of the answers it brings. Each floating fish is eyed with suspicion and added to a tally that no one kept count of before.

As rumors of the boy's death spread across the sea, boats stop coming to shore. Surrounding islanders worry that the stars are hiding in the daylight. They fear the contagion of a night-lit sea. They stop visiting, stop trading with the island for supplies. The last of them brings only word. He shouts from beyond the shallows to say that they'll be back soon enough. They'll stay gone for only as long as it takes for the light to fade, he says. But for the islanders hemmed in by menace and beauty, the stars are present and lingering and possibly forever.

*

When their habitat grows hostile (a shift in temperature or light; high predation), the plankton adopt a different reproductive strategy. A new cell hatches and sinks to the ocean floor. It burrows into sediment, lies in wait, sometimes for years: a seed, ready to germinate. These can be carried by current or animal and dispersed to new environments. Given opportune conditions, the plankton will bloom again.

*

Rafa begins to lose track of the daytime. He sleeps and wakes in reverse, and time blurs in between. He feels a brush of lips on his forehead, the rocking of his hammock, or else nothing at all. When he wakes, he is always alone.

One evening, he wakes to find the glass bowl returned to his bedside. Someone has carried it back to him—someone who knows that the bowl is his. The stars inside swim in near synchronization, in one direction and then another. Light dances across the walls. Rafa casts the patterns over memories of skin, and the thought lulls him back to sleep.

Rafa wakes again in darkness. He sits up to search for a match. He strikes one and lights the candle beside his bed, and there is the bowl, full and still. He taps it and watches the liquid inside shudder. It stays clear. The stars do not compete for light, and so

Rafa blows the candle out. The scent of wicksmoke slips through the hut, which remains as dark as night.

Rafa feels for the glass's rim. He plunges a finger into the bowl and meets water, waits for the specks of light to cluster around it—around him. When nothing comes but damp and cold, he lifts his finger out. Rafa brings it to his lips. He pauses, then flicks out his tongue to taste. Water drips down his palm and into the crook of his arm. The bowl is dark, its contents inert. Rafa lies back. He probes with his tongue for light, for stars in the darkness. He tastes only the thick salinity of home and of himself.

AIR SHIFTS

A **WOMAN CALLS IN WITH A** hunch about her husband.
Go right ahead, says Jack.

He's screwing around, she says—she's almost sure of it—with someone he works with, or someone from their son's T-ball team, which is especially low-down, she says, because she *knows* those women, even brings in grapes and juice boxes for their little sluggers. Because she's happy to, of course, but also so she can keep an eye on her husband, who coaches the team—so she can see whose mommy might be paying him *too* much attention, or which one seems the unhappiest to see her there, or which one looks like the biggest hussy.

Well, says the caller, *Brenda* looks like the biggest hussy, but it isn't her he's sleeping with. Poor girl loves a cheetah print. But she's not his type.

Catfight at the T-ball field! says Bubba. He plays a sound effect, strays yowling and hissing.

Sounds like a nice guy—this husband of yours, says Jack.

Coaching Little Leaguers and the like. What makes you think he's cheating?

He's home later than he used to be, says the caller, for one. When he does pull up, he heads straight upstairs and takes a shower.

A shower? says Jack.

A shower—first thing. Doesn't hardly say hello, she says. Even brushes his teeth before he comes down. Like he's washing the scent of her off, whoever she is.

You think she stinks? says Bubba.

I wouldn't know, now would I? says the caller. He even tosses his clothes in the laundry and he *never* used to do that, she says. Believe me—I've asked.

This man gets cleaner and more helpful by the minute, says Bubba. The dog!

Ma'am, says Jack. I'd like to ask you a few questions if that's all right.

Go right ahead, says the caller.

Your husband—when he's home—is he fidgety?

He's twitchy, all right. Probably 'cause I'm catchin' on, she says.

Mm-hmm. And has he gotten thinner since all this started? I really hate to think of him getting fit for someone else.

Or fitting *in* to someone else, says Bubba.

Goodness, says the woman.

Not so fast, says Jack. Is he buying flashy stuff—new clothes or shoes?

Nothing like that, but he could stand to. He's hopeless in the fashion department—still wears all the shirts and ties me and the kids buy him for Christmas.

Where you headed with this, buddy? says Bubba.

It's like this, says Jack. I got a hunch of my own, and if my suspicions are correct—and mind you, I've been wrong before—your husband's *indiscretions* aren't to do with another woman at all.

Go on? says the woman.

Jack waits for a beat, though the light's started blinking to show it's time to play a song. I hate to be the one to tell you, ma'am—

Tell *her*? Tell the rest of us! says Bubba.

But it sounds like your husband's picked up nothin' more than a smoking habit.

Bubba busts out laughing.

Ma'am? says Jack.

There's a sound over the air like Bubba slapping his knee. That no-good liar's stepping out with none other than a cigarette! he says.

You still there? says Jack, but she isn't.

Jack and Bubba on the case again! says Bubba. Call in to call out!

They cut to "I Heard It Through the Grapevine" by Creedence Clearwater Revival.

Tabitha has a caller on the line who's going through a professional crisis. She calls it that, the caller: a crisis.

Tell me about it, honey, says Tabitha.

I just worry, says the caller, I'm wasting up all my potential. I've got dreams, you know? But those take time to get after—and energy—and I don't have a drop of it left after I get home.

Worn out, says Tabitha. I've been there.

Runnin' copy after copy at the office, says the caller. Chasing down so-and-so's paperwork for such-and-such to sign. And then there's another company birthday—another cake to buy for a grown adult that I've gotta pick up and cut up and sing over, wearing flats that skin up the backs of my heels when I'd rather just be home. After that, all I've got is tired, Tabitha. All I've got is waiting for the weekend, and then it starts up again.

I hear you. A happy birthday for everyone but you, sounds like, says Tabitha. But tell me, honey: What's the thing you'd do if you could? That big, wild dream. Let's air it out.

The caller says her dream's not so big, not so wild. She says she wants to go back to school, study speech therapy. Says her son's got a stutter and she barely has the time to help him through it.

It's the *T*'s and *D*'s that give him trouble, the caller says. Just gets hung up. Gets so frustrated it could break your heart, which only makes it worse for him, getting spun up like that. He's a real smart kid. Just needs a little more patience than most.

I'll bet he is, Tabitha says. Sounds brave too. Like his mother.

The caller sniffles. That means a lot to hear you say it, she says.

Now you listen to me, says Tabitha. This life is hard, and the best things don't come easy. But you let your dream guide you—let it light you up and take you where you want to be.

Where I wanna be, says the caller—like she's committing it to memory.

I'm dedicating this next song to you, honey, Tabitha says. Keep that precious flame alight. May it give you strength.

She cuts to "Girl on Fire" by Alicia Keys.

Jack and Bubba get a caller who's quit his job.

Where at? says Jack.

Over at the Pop 'n Shop on Denver.

Sure sure, says Bubba. Wife says I've gotta stay off those boiled peanuts y'all keep pipin' hot, but I just can't help myself.

Trust me on this one, says the caller. She's right. Steer clear of those things. We don't change out the old ones—just dump the new batch right on top.

Like seasoning to a cast iron, my friend, says Bubba. My mouth's watering as we speak.

He's droolin', folks, says Jack.

My lucky spot for scratchers, too, says Bubba. That place has it all!

That's what you think, says the caller. You ever won big?

Not yet, says Bubba. I'm lettin' the luck build up.

Figures, says the caller.

What made you quit, friend? says Jack.

Yeah, give us the dirt, says Bubba. Go right ahead.

Just got tired of it, says the caller. Same thing day in, day out—same old, same old.

We wouldn't know anything about that, says Jack.

Nothin' at all, says Bubba. Not us.

Plus, my boss was always riding my case—sending me in to

scrub the toilets, even when it wasn't my turn. You know what people do to gas station bathrooms?

Nothing good, I'd guess, says Jack.

I'm not dealing with it, says the caller. Not my problem anymore. No sir. Not me.

You got something else lined up? says Jack.

Sure don't and bills to pay, says the caller. Bills to pay, he repeats—stretching the words out longer. Then, Y'all hirin'?

You wouldn't make it here, either, pal, says Bubba. Our toilets really need seeing to, after I get through with 'em.

They cut to Bon Jovi's "Livin' on a Prayer."

Tabitha wants to talk about rumors. She says they almost always do more harm than good.

Now I don't know about that, says a caller with a counterpoint. We all gotta let off some steam every once in a while. No harm in a little gossip.

I'm all about a release, says Tabitha, but keep it healthy, honey. Take a walk, take a bath. Buy something nice for yourself. Punch a pillow if need be, but a line of gossip shreds the town. My mother used to say that. You can't pick yourself up with someone else's fall.

Well, *I* sure can, says the caller. Especially if it's somethin' good. She laughs. Don't get all high and mighty on me, Tabitha. You've never heard a rumor so good you just had to tell someone else?

I rein the impulse in, says Tabitha.

Well, good on you, says the caller. Tabitha the saint. Not me. Personally, I *believe* in gossip. Hasn't let me down once.

Not that you know of, maybe.

The caller carries on like she didn't hear. Lotta times, she says, there's at least an ounce of truth to it. Like, listen to this: there was this youth group leader at my church growing up. Theo. All the girls woulda died for him. Hot Theo. *Bodacious* Theo. If we worshipped any false idols, it was him. He wore his hair long and loose, kept it pushed outta his face with a pair of aviators, like some kind of Top Gun Jesus.

Danger zone, warns Tabitha.

You bet, says the caller. And there was talk that once you got confirmed, Theo would bless you with a kiss on the cheek. Nothing too serious, but they said he'd get right up next to you, smelling like Old Spice or Axe, or whatever it was he wore. Probably something horrible but if I smell it now, it still brings up that same old feeling.

The caller pauses for a moment, perhaps in reverie.

Let's just say we all found our way to God, she says. Though I'll say at least *I* never got that kiss.

A faithful flock, says Tabitha.

Oh, come on, Tabitha. Judge not, remember? There's more to it, is what I'm saying. A couple years after I went off to college, my mother called to tell me Hot Theo left the church. No particular reason—just up and moved. But everybody knew. That there's the power of gossip, Tabitha. Held a speck of truth.

But listen, honey, says Tabitha. What if someone had brought that little scandal out into the light rather than let it fester? Rather than let it lurk around in the dark? Don't you think it could've made a difference?

At Holy Redeemer? says the caller. Not likely. We loved our

secrets. Kept 'em just to have 'em, sometimes. What's the point of repentance if you're always good? Might as well earn it. The caller pauses to laugh. You're not Catholic, are you, Tabitha?

Gossip is a coward's truth, is my point. I won't see it any other way.

Tabitha cuts to Michael Jackson's "Man in the Mirror."

Hi there, says a caller on the line. This is Shasta. I'm calling in regards to your Volkswagen warranty.

Here we go, says Jack.

I hate these, says Bubba. All day, every day. What kind of name is Shasta, even?

Like the soda, says Jack.

Right. I wonder what made 'em choose that—a common, run-of-the-mill name like Shasta, says Jack. Here to help me out with a VW Bug I don't even *have*, by the way. Not sure where they're getting their intel.

Jack presses the horn button on the soundboard—a feeble *beep beep!* Let's let it play out this time, he says. For *research*.

. . . congratulate you on your one-thousand-dollar instant rebate—

I finally won something! says Bubba.

Congrats, buddy! Now all she'll need is your Social Security number to make it happen.

Just call me back to redeem this special, onetime offer.

Say what you will, but Shasta's really sellin' this, says Bubba.

You heard the lady, says Jack.

They dial the number on air. It rings twice and picks up.

Hello, says a male voice, and thank you for calling to discuss this exciting offer! Who do I have the pleasure of speaking with today?

Hold up now—this ain't Shasta, says Bubba.

No, sir, says the other line. She's out sick today. You're speaking with her manager, Jeffrey. I'm happy to help, Mr. . . . ?

You're on with *Jack and Bubba in the Morning*, says Jack. Live on the air. We're wondering if you might give the people a taste of what it is you're *really* selling.

The other line is quiet. There's a cough somewhere in the background, the sound of landlines ringing.

Jeffrey? Jeff? says Bubba.

Jeffrey doesn't answer, but there's a sound like scratching at the receiver—a rustling against it.

Since we've got you here, says Bubba, I'm wondering how it is y'all do the thing with area codes? I get a call from my buddy who lives outta town, and then there y'all are not a minute later, calling with a number from the same place. Magic.

Jeff? You there, man? says Jack.

There's a sound like the phone's been dropped, and then he's back.

It seems there's been a mistake, sir, he says. Er—sirs. Thank you for calling and good evening.

The line goes dead.

You think he knows it's eight a.m.? says Bubba.

Nice guy, says Jack. No *Shasta*, but—

Their line lights up with another call.

No way, says Jack. Not back-to-back!

Time is running out! says a pre-recorded voice when they answer.
They play Dead or Alive's "You Spin Me Round."

Tabitha's caller just lost her father.

I'm so sorry to hear that, says Tabitha. The loss of a parent is a terrible thing. How long's it been?

We just put him in the ground this afternoon.

Oh, goodness.

I'm driving back from my momma's house now, says the caller. She's a wreck.

So fresh.

Excuse me? says the caller, hiccuping.

The grief, I mean. The pain. That's all I meant.

Tabitha pauses.

Honey, she says, I wonder if we might be able to strike up a little magic for you right now. I wonder if you'd tell me a favorite memory of your father. He may be gone, but you can keep him alive in your heart, just by remembering.

A memory? says the caller.

Just one. You think of one today, and another tomorrow, and you go on just like that.

I can't think of anything good, says the caller. Just . . . all I can see—over and over—is his body.

His—

Mama *insisted* on an open casket. Said we needed to see him one last time. Say goodbye before they put him under. And they did a good job, I guess, says the caller. I guess that's a thing people say. They smoothed him out with something. Looked almost inflated. Not *puffy*, exactly. But full. He looked, maybe, ten years younger? Not sure why they do that. Last place you need youth is a grave.

The caller pauses.

At least he didn't look sick, she says.

Oh, honey, says Tabitha.

But now, says the caller, it's like the last time I saw him is all I've got. I keep picturing him just like that, laid out in a coffin.

Oh goodness, says Tabitha again. She is normally very good at knowing what to say. Her callers rely on her for it.

How long till I can remember him the way he was?

The caller waits, but the line stays quiet.

How long till I forget how he is now—right now? she tries. Puffed up and spoilin' in the dirt.

It just takes time, says Tabitha. I'm sorry.

How much time? The caller's voice is tight.

I wish I could tell you. I really do.

Please? she begs.

Grief can be abundant, says Tabitha, but so is love. You remember that, honey. So is love.

She cuts to "Nothing Compares 2 U" by Sinéad O'Connor.

The studio brings in Mimi sometimes, to offer *Jack and Bubba in the Morning* a feminine perspective.

Now, Mimi, says Bubba. You're a woman.

Thank God, says Mimi.

What is it—in your expert opinion—that women want?

And why won't they just come out and say it? says the caller on the line.

Well, I don't know if you've heard, says Mimi, but men aren't always the best listeners.

What? says Bubba. Come again?

The caller laughs, and Mimi does too.

So even if we say it outright, she says, y'all are usually too hardheaded to hear it.

Probably evolutionary, says the caller. If you believe in that sort of thing.

So why waste our breath? says Mimi.

To loop us in, that's why, says Jack—a bit too loudly into the mic.

A little hint is all I'm looking for, says Bubba. You wouldn't believe how much wax is built up in these ears.

The caller laughs.

How are we supposed to know what y'all are after? says Jack.

Listeners have come to expect flirtation between him and Mimi. That's how it's always played out before.

All the *mystery*, Jack says now—his tone a little meaner today. All the thinkin' you do about something till it's picked dry. What good does that do?

Be professional, Jack, says Mimi.

Y'all good? says Bubba.

What is it women like in bed? says the caller.

Otherwise you're just waiting for us to fail, says Jack. Right?

Sure, Jack, says Mimi. That's what I was doing.

That sure is what it feels like, says Jack.

Okay, buddy, says Bubba. Calm down. Let's just calm down. We're all friends here.

Friends is right, says Jack. Apparently that's all we are.

Everyone's got a limit, Jack, says Mimi. Everybody wears out. So that's it? End of story?

Am I missing something? says the caller.

I *told* them not to schedule me anymore, says Mimi.

Well, here you are, says Jack.

I said, put me on with Tabitha. Boy, have I got a story to tell her.

I swear—Jack starts.

Now, buddy, warns Bubba, let's not say anything we're gonna regret. We got a show to do.

I thought y'all were cute together, says the caller.

They cut to "Barracuda" by Heart.

It's the Lovely Hour—a staple of *The Talk with Tabitha*, a specialty. She plays Bill Withers's "Lovely Day" in the background. Listeners call in with their most pressing dilemmas and heartbreaks, and Tabitha sets them straight. She's a shoulder to lean on. A safe space. A soothsayer for the broken hearts of Lauderdale County and the surrounding valley. She leads those astray back to themselves.

A young man calls in to tell Tabitha how much her show means to him.

Really, he says. I'm not just blowing smoke. There've been days where I just have to hear you, when I tune in to get a little dose of your advice. You're my medicine, Tabitha.

Bless you for that, she says. It means the world to me—it really does. It's you all who keep me afloat.

I mean every bit. It's not just for moms—I don't care what people say.

You heard it here first, folks, she says. *The Talk with Tabitha*: not just for moms.

You've pulled me out of some dark holes, says the caller. Your voice basically put me through college.

I'm glad to hear it, honey. And here you are on the Lovely Hour, where the topic of the hour is love. What can I help you with?

I guess that *is* the bit, huh? Call in, spill your guts.

Spill 'em, honey.

I can't believe I'm doing this, he says. But—okay. Say you have someone you love dearly.

Lucky you, says Tabitha.

Lucky me, says the caller. And this someone: he's truly your partner. You're barely apart, but you don't mind it.

Just one look at you, sings Bill Withers.

Some days, says the caller, he falls asleep on the sofa after a workout, all sweaty with the cat curled up on his chest. And you'd hate that with anyone else, on the furniture like that—it's disgusting. And you should tell him to wake up and take a shower. Stop stinking up the place. But there's light streaming in through the windows, and you're just struck dumb standing there, staring at him—trying not to move or wake him up. And it feels perfect. Like . . .

The caller searches for a moment.

It feels like a memory, he says, even while it's happening right there in front of you.

Honey, says Tabitha. I've gotta tell you—I'm tearing up. Tabitha cries, or says she does, at least once per show. Every evening, for the last decade, she gets misty on air.

I'm sure I'm not the only one blubbering, she says. What you two have sounds special. Like paradise. How long have y'all been together?

A couple months, but it feels longer.

A love to undo time.

Right, says the caller. But say there's the *slightest* issue. Pales in comparison to the rest of it. But still.

Every engine needs a tune-up, honey. Even one that's running smoothly.

Exactly, says the caller.

Let's hear it then.

Okay. So, say this person—the love of your life—lacks in just one department. Or . . . lacks isn't the right word. Maybe the opposite.

Uh-oh, honey. What are we talking about here?

Don't worry, says the caller. I know it's radio. I'll be good, Tabitha.

Be good, she says.

The Talk with Tabitha gives obscenity a wide berth.

Let's say, says the caller, your beloved isn't necessarily *receptive*. Generous, but not receptive.

Tabitha clears her throat.

Say if I'm trying to provide a certain—let's call it—*happiness* for my partner—my other half—and they respond by saying, Thanks but no thanks.

Now, we might have to hop off here, honey, but communication is key—

You start to wonder if maybe you're doing something wrong, Tabitha—you know what I mean? Maybe there's a *reason* they're turning your offers down, but they love you too much to say so.

Let me leave you with this, says Tabitha. If we go looking for problems, we're more than likely to find them.

This doesn't happen to me, Tabitha. It's not like I've heard this before.

Perfect takes time, honey. A problem is just an opportunity to grow.

I've been listening to you for years, Tabitha, says the caller. I love you.

I love you, too, honey.

But if you could just come right out and say it, this one time, says the caller, it would really help me out.

We naturally turn toward light, says Tabitha. Toward what brings us peace. Even pleasure. We rarely confuse that light for darkness.

Lovely day, lovely day, sings Bill.

I'm probably just bad at it—is that what you're saying? I'm bringing the darkness while he's, you know, lighting me up?

Grow together and glow together, says Tabitha. Thanks for calling in, and best of luck to both of you.

She cuts the call.

I do love to hear from my longtime listeners, Tabitha says. You're my family. We're all in this together.

She cuts to "Hungry Eyes" by Eric Carmen.

Jack and Bubba are doing a segment. Throughout the week, their team drops topics into a spittoon they keep in the studio. The spittoon is stickered with a label that reads DON'T SPIT. Today's topic is hair loss.

Now, I don't have a lick of hair up top, says Bubba.

Folks, you can't see this, says Jack, but he ain't lyin. He's got his hat off for once and I can see my reflection clear as day, right off the top of his dome. And *boy* do I look good!

You know mirrors can distort an image, right? Objects may be uglier than they appear?

Aw, I know you don't mean that, buddy. I won't take it personal.

What's your secret then, Jack? For those luscious locks of yours?

A deal with the devil. Good genes, I guess. My daddy went to his grave with a full head of hair.

Lucky duck, says Bubba.

Lucky, says Jack. Sure. Forty years old and gone too soon, but not a bald spot on 'im.

Aw, Jack, I wasn't thinking. I forgot.

No harm done, says Jack. You know I'm turning forty-two in May?

That doesn't mean—

You know my momma says I'm his spitting image? Whoa! Jack says, realizing he's made a pun. He plays the sound effect that sounds like someone's hocking a loogie.

Bubba laughs half-heartedly.

Momma says it's like he rose up outta the grave, lookin' at me, says Jack. Lately she mentions it near every time she has a few drinks. Can't seem to help it. Spittin' image of my long-dead daddy, she says, as long as I've got my hair.

We'll be back after a short break, folks.

They play "Only the Good Die Young" by Billy Joel.

Tabitha's got a caller on the line who's distraught. They always come to her distraught. She blames the time slot and the calming ochre of her voice.

I think my husband's been unfaithful, says the caller.

I'm so sorry to hear it, says Tabitha. What makes you think so?

Well, he said he was, says the caller. He confessed.

Tabitha misses a beat.

It's just—he's a good man, Tabitha. He could never.

You—you don't believe him?

How could I? He's such a good father, always looking out for me and the girls. No signs of it either—not that I could tell.

Oh, honey, Tabitha says. Why would he lie about a thing like that?

He's my *husband*, Tabitha. That's gotta count for *something*.

When someone tells you who they are, believe them, says

Tabitha. Maya Angelou said that—a hero of mine. A strong woman who didn't have the easiest of time with men, either, but—

What do you know, anyway? says the caller. You're divorced.

Tabitha cuts to "Believe" by Cher.

Jack says he's looking to broaden his horizons.

Look here, he says. Things are all right. Not too bad. I get to come in here every morning and talk to my buddy Bubba.

That's me! I'm the buddy, says Bubba.

And all of you lovely people, too. Talk about the good, the bad.

Don't forget the ugly, says Bubba.

The ugly, right. Me and Bubba here, we play some tunes. Play our little show into the airwaves.

That's *Jack and Bubba in the Morning*, folks. Call in to call out!

And then I pick up and I go home, says Jack, and we do it all again.

It really is as good as it sounds, is what he's saying.

That's what I'm saying. But I drive outta here, right? says Jack. I pick up a sub sandwich on the way home. I sit down, I eat it. I watch a little TV. Run some errands, maybe. I fix dinner, have a beer. Watch a little more TV. And then I go to bed.

Ain't nothin' wrong with it, says Bubba. What you're describing right there sounds like bliss.

That right? says Jack.

Paradise. Between the kids and the dogs and Cathy, every day at the Bubba residence is something new.

Bubba's your last name?

What'd you think it was?

They laugh.

No, but really, says Jack. I could use some of what you've got.

I barely make it outta there alive, buddy, says Bubba.

Sure.

I mean it. Ain't two days the same. You know the other week, Becca says she won't eat food anymore that's not the color orange. You believe that? Just a ploy to not have to eat anything besides Goldfish, if you ask me. I was a kid once. I know the tricks. But she's sticking to it.

What made her pick orange? says Jack. That's carrots. Count me right out on carrots.

The other night I said, You're not leaving this table till you clear your plate—I don't care what color's on it. And dadgummit if she didn't fall asleep at the dinner table.

Well, you've gotta admire her conviction, says Jack.

I haven't seen that kid eat anything but orange for three weeks, Bubba says. She's got us packing orange lunches so she doesn't starve to death at school. She's got us *whipped*.

Bubba presses the correlating button on the soundboard for emphasis.

But that's life, is what I mean, Jack says. That's living, what you're doing.

Trust me, says Bubba. It's another leak in the roof and a hole in your pocket and an ulcer in your gut and a billion things you gotta remember, but won't. Me? I'd take simple. Give me a week of routine, Jack. And that sandwich while you're at it.

Bubba laughs. Jack laughs.

All I'm saying is I could do with a little chaos, maybe. Could be good for me.

Your life ain't empty, pal, says Bubba. It's roomy. Room to breathe.

Says you.

Says me.

They play "You Can't Always Get What You Want" by the Rolling Stones.

Tabitha is running a segment on joy. She would like more people to call in joyfully. In the midst of joy.

Joy is something we all have to cultivate, says Tabitha. Every single day. It doesn't just come to us, or come for us. We plant the seed. We water it.

There's a slow saxophone track playing in the background while she talks.

You've gotta come back to see where the joy has sprouted in your life—not always where you'd expect. We've got a caller on the line now. Go ahead, honey.

There's quiet.

Looks like they got cut off, says Tabitha.

She moves closer to the mic.

Talk joy with me today, folks. Bring your joys to me.

The saxophone plays on its own—doleful, smooth.

It could be the day, folks, but I still think it's important to commemorate joy—maybe even more so—on a day like today. A day of national tragedy. Never forget, they say, but we carry on. We find joy nonetheless.

The track picks up, the sax a little bolder now.

I think you've gotta look for it everywhere. Every chance you get, America.

She cuts to "Calling All Angels" by Train.

You're in a good mood today, says Jack.

I guess I am, says Bubba.

You get laid or something? says the caller on the line.

It's nothin', says Bubba.

No, please—share with the group, says Jack.

Go right ahead, says the caller. In *detail*, he adds.

It's my kid, says Bubba.

Oh, says the caller.

You know she's been sick, says Bubba.

I do. I do, buddy, says Jack.

My little Savannah. Our trouper, plugged into all those tubes and beeping and smiling at me and her momma like nothing's the matter.

Sweet Savannah, says Jack.

Jeez, says the caller. I didn't mean to—

We just found out—just last night, they confirmed it. She's gettin' better, says Bubba. Stronger every day, it seems like. They ran their tests and it's in remission, finally. She's runnin' that bastard off.

A censor flickers.

Great news, buddy, says Jack. Give her my love, will you?

Mine, too, says the caller. Bless you, brave Savannah.

Bubba dissolves to gentle sobs, and the caller clears his throat. They cut to Van Morrison's "Brown Eyed Girl."

Is this Mrs. Moran? says a caller on the line.

You're on with Tabitha, says Tabitha, who is neither a Moran nor a Mrs. any longer, who will need to pronounce Ms. with a hard z from now on so that people catch her drift and quickly.

How can I help? says Tabitha, who is happy to share the details of herself with her audience—her heart, the show's tender center—but can't stand to hear a surname that isn't hers on air, though it still belongs to the child she carried into this world, and though it still accosts her on daily mail: invitations and Christmas cards and junk catalogs, addressed to a former version of herself. How strange to have shed half her identity. How strange to have given part of herself away in the first place.

Ma'am, we've been trying to reach you, says the caller. It's Ricky. Your son, Ricky. This is Coach B calling.

Is Ricky all right? says Tabitha.

Ricky's having some *behavioral* issues today, says Coach B. Needs someone to come pick him up from practice.

Faintly, in the background, she hears Ricky say, I *told* you not to call her. Tabitha wonders if her listeners heard it too.

That's fine, says Tabitha. Thank you, she says. Let me call you right back.

She hangs up the line, and surely there's a producer who's due an earful, or some intern whose job it is at the very least to watch Tabitha's cell phone and field any calls that might be urgent, so some do-good coach doesn't call in to make her son sound violent, make Tabitha seem unfit—the unfit mother of a violent Black child. Though it's not even clear to Tabitha if her listeners know she's Black. She can usually tell hearing someone's voice over the phone, but she hardly ever mentions race—hers or others'—outright on air, and with the questions some of them call in with—the *audacity* of some of them—she's not quite sure. No, a call from some coach is not what she needs, especially when it isn't even her week with Ricky—when it's his father's week, though the school might not be looped in to this particular detail and though she's likely listed first as the emergency contact. They wouldn't have listened to Ricky saying, *Not my mom—she's busy*, or else they *did* listen to Ricky, who gave them the direct number to call her on air, out of spite or because it is the easiest to remember, from the way she repeats it singsong at the top of every half hour.

To her listeners, she says only, Kids. It's always something new, isn't it?

She laughs. They are in on the joke together, Tabitha and her listeners.

The blessing of children is they keep us on our toes and an inch closer to heaven that way. She says, You'll be right back on with *The Talk with Tabitha* after ten uninterrupted songs in a row, and she cuts to "I Don't Want to Miss a Thing" by Aerosmith.

Jack says he thinks he's losing his mind.

Oh, it's *long* gone, says Bubba.

Too late, says the caller.

No, really, Jack says. Every day, it's something else. You ever have that thing happen to you where you walk into a room and forget why you're there?

You know what I do? says the caller. It's a little tip my shrink gave me. Yeah—that's right. I've been to *therapy*, before y'all say something smart. I'm what you might call an evolved man.

Get on with it then, says Bubba.

I just keep whispering what the thing is I'm in there for, says the caller. Creates intention, my therapist says, which I am then able to man-i-fest.

Bubba presses the button on their soundboard that says, *Oh, brother!*

Give it a try, Jack, says the caller. My advice to you—no charge. Walk into a room saying *scissors, scissors*, and it's hard to forget what you're there for.

But the next problem is, says Bubba, everyone else in the room thinks you're a lunatic.

That's the risk you take, says the caller. But at least you can cut 'em up if you flip the switch.

The caller laughs. Bubba laughs.

But listen, says Jack. It's bigger than that. My sister just got married, right? Nice guy, good to her. Name of Henry—easy enough. Well, goshdarnit if I don't call him Steve every time I see him. She's never even dated a Steve. But I take one look at him and that's all there is. Every time.

Hardly sounds like a medical condition, says Bubba.

The man might just look like a Steve, says the caller. Maybe you've got it right, and his own momma got it wrong.

Or, I had to set up security questions for my banking password the other day, says Jack—talking fast. And I can't remember any of the right stuff. Not the name of the street I grew up on or my first-grade teacher, or even the name of my first best buddy before we moved away.

Everybody has trouble with those, says Bubba. Just write it down.

I'm saying, I only know the wrong stuff. That buddy—his family had this huge chocolate Labrador. Kept her in a pen in the yard. Cookie. Never got a walk, hardly ever got let out. Used to jump up on the fence and go berserk anytime we got near her. Just too excited, too big—too *lonely*, I guess—for us to play with her. I always wanted to sneak in and set Cookie free. I was scared of her, though, deep down. And she stank.

Poor Cookie, says the caller.

I can remember all that, is what I'm saying. I can picture Cookie, right now. But the kid's name? What *he* looked like? Gone. What do you call that?

Might have a weak spot for human names, says Bubba.

It's more than that, says Jack. All I've got is useless stuff. Little moments, feelings. Like, I was pukin' up carrots at the airport once as a kid, and my mom needed us to get to the gate. She puts the handles of a shopping bag over my ears so I could barf and walk at the same time. We board the plane and I'm still puking and the flight attendant gives me a cup of ginger ale, which I thought for the longest time after was medicine. All that is crystal clear. I don't mess with carrots to this day. But—where were we going? Where were we coming from? Couldn't tell you.

I'll have to try that bag trick sometime, says Bubba. Right over the ears, next hangover.

Sometimes, says Jack, I'm having a drink with a buddy and he'll say, Hey, remember the time when we did such-and-such with so-and-so? And I laugh along, but I've got nothing. Zip. Just a hole where the memory should be. Like my body's been dragging around to all these places without me.

Uh, Jack? says Bubba, his tone mock-serious. You, uh, remember who I am, don't you?

Jack sighs. Unfortunately, he says.

And me? says the caller.

No one here knows you, friend, says Bubba.

Fair, says the caller.

And, Jack? says Bubba. You do remember what it is we do here, right?

I remember, says Jack. Absolutely nothing. Sittin' here doing nothin', talking about even less.

You got it, buddy, says Bubba. Seems like you've got a grip to me.

Try the scissors thing, says the caller. Just give it a go. Might help.

They cut to "Slip Slidin' Away" by Paul Simon.

You're on with Tabitha. Speak your truth.

Oh, Tabby, says the caller. I lost my dog.

No one's called me that in a long time, she says—though she

might wish to correct him instead, to say that her name and the show's are the same three, deliberate syllables. Just Tabitha, she'd say. That's it.

I'm sorry to hear it, though, honey, she says. The loss of a pet can be a terrible thing. Like losing a family member.

That's the thing, says the caller. My wife left me, too. I thought she'd gone to look for him, but she ain't come back yet, either.

How long's it been since she left?

All night, says the caller.

Oh my. Are you sure she's all right?

Tabitha would not classify most of her calls as emergencies, though once, a very sad woman called in, talking about how she wanted to *leave this cruel world*. At the time, Tabitha had thought the phrase sounded melodramatic—thin—but the caller kept repeating herself until it sounded threatening. Possible. Tabitha did what she could to soothe her, but she wasn't *that* kind of professional. She couldn't have it on her conscience if she had made things any worse. Tabitha kept the woman talking and called the police, had the woman in one ear and the dispatcher in the other, until she managed to get the caller's address (*Yes, honey, but where exactly are you leaving the world from?*). Now, Tabitha gives the suicide prevention hotline every Sunday evening during her slot, which is when she's determined people are at their saddest.

Can you think of anywhere she might be—your wife? says Tabitha now. Anywhere you can think of to look for her?

Well, that's the other thing, says the caller, barely holding it together now. She took my truck, so I lost that, too. My truck, my girl, *and* my best hound dog!

He snorts into his receiver, then the line goes dead.

You think I need this, folks? says Tabitha.

She cuts to "I'm the Only One" by Melissa Etheridge.

Y'all will never believe what I got myself into, says a caller, and then another. Hijinks are Jack and Bubba's bread and butter—their own, others. Any number of callers have reported any number of misfortunes over the years. Bubba says his wife thinks he must *try* to get himself into trouble, with as often as he finds himself caught up in it.

I don't, though! he says. I swear it. Just lucky in being unlucky.

Last month, Bubba tried to sell his boat on Craigslist, had a guy drive out to meet him at their country house to see it.

He wanted to meet at night was the first sign, says Bubba when he's ready to talk about it. Shoulda guessed something was up. Who can get a good look at a fishing boat in the dark? Bubba got there and parked and pulled the tarp off the boat, scrubbed some rust off the trailer. But the guy was late, didn't show up for a long while.

I guess in retrospect, says Bubba, he just wanted the address. But I wasn't too mad about it. *Opportunity for some peace and quiet,* I thought. And there were cold beers in the fridge. I set out on the porch and had me one or two, and then after a couple hours, a truck pulls up and I think, *All right, probably got lost on the way in.* I think, *Service coulda been bad so he didn't get my texts, neither.* He cuts off his headlights in the driveway and I think, *That's the least he can do—keep 'em from shining in my eyes.* But the guy climbed out looking scared as hell to see me there, and him the one with the gun.

The caller gasps.

Jack has heard the story before, but he still says, Unbelievable.

Bubba says maybe on account of the shock of it, or the beer, it took him a while to register what was happening—that the guy was holding a gun, pointing it at him, walking up on him. He wasn't even shouting or swearing at Bubba. Seemed like the soft-spoken type, nervous. Bubba says the guy was wearing a black shirt with LEE COUNTY WIND ENSEMBLE printed on the chest, which did not, to Bubba, seem to be the mark of a criminal mastermind.

I got held up by a dang band geek, says Bubba.

Bubba says after it was over—after he'd climbed into the guy's truck, driver's side, at gunpoint and backed it up and hitched up the trailer for him, still at gunpoint, and then watched him drive off—not even that fast, since it's not so easy to peel off with a trailer and a boat hitched to you—Bubba just drove himself home. He says once he'd caught Cathy up to speed, she went, in Bubba's estimation, *ballistic* about it and sent him right back out to file a police report with her on the phone in his ear, reminding him of the details he'd told her and then just as soon forgotten.

But Bubba said the thing itself—the robbery—hadn't gone at all the way he thought it might've, wasn't anything like the movies. He didn't try to get away or wrestle the gun loose, or anything. Bubba says everything slowed up and he could see every detail clear—could hear his own heartbeat in his ears. All's he could think about was getting home to his girls.

No action star, after all, I guess, says Bubba. Just a family man now. Just somebody's daddy. Cathy woulda been pissed, too, if I'd died over a boat she warned me not to buy in the first place.

Bubba laughs. The caller laughs.

Jack says, I sure am glad you're okay, buddy.

He says, When I think about what could've happened . . .

He says, I'd be lost on here without you.

They cut to "Wild World" by Cat Stevens.

Tabitha is on hiatus. They play her greatest hits—recordings of when she talked her listeners out of their darkest times. They called in about their heartbreaks, their missed chances, the trials they'd faced and lost. Together it was easy to be earnest—to be hurt and torn through, and then sewn back together by Tabitha—her wise words, her faith that they would muster through it.

Tabitha, says a caller, I don't think he's coming back.

You'll carry on, says Tabitha. You're your own best thing, and the only one who'll never leave you.

Tabitha, says a caller, how could anyone be so awful?

Some folks are just broken. Just aren't right. Some people have the wind blowing through them.

Tabitha is so close in the old episodes, so open. She shares the details of her wedding day—how the buttercream in her cake tasted spoiled somehow, soured, maybe by the heat, but they ate it anyway. She talks about the first apartment she ever bought— all by herself—just to have a place of her own that no one could take from her. She filled up every inch of wall space, she says, with picture frames. Her parents and family. Tabitha and friends, arms wrapped around one another, smiles bright.

I couldn't have been lonely there if I'd tried, she says.

Tabitha loses a pregnancy, gains a son. Her husband trickles away from her, and though she doesn't announce it till the very end, you can hear it if you're really listening—to what she says, and to the hollowed-out spaces where she's quiet, where the mic captures a background track churning on its own, turning static to song.

No new calls play on air now, though perhaps the phone is ringing—lines blinking on and off, trying to break their way through.

We've got another treat for you this evening, folks, says a voice that isn't Tabitha's. A dry voice—male. A poor substitute. Why would they pick a man to fill in for her?

It's the best of *The Talk with Tabitha*, says the voice, all night long for your listening pleasure.

Hours of her loop, and she calls her listeners honey. She calls them baby. She says they can't be alone if they have each other—if they have Tabitha, and she has them.

They play "Have I Told You Lately."

They play "Because You Loved Me."

They play "How Am I Supposed to Live Without You."

If she's coming back, it's not tonight, and the tracks play on without her.

DECENCY RULE

THE MAYOR TOLD US NOT to wear clothes anymore.

It was really a crazy thing for him to say. We couldn't believe it.

No one thought he'd make it into office and then no one thought he'd make it one year and then two, and then there we were in his third term, and he told us to strip down. At first, we thought it was a bad joke. Our mayors had never been sensational before, but this mayor often was. We'd grown accustomed to outrage.

At the press conference, the mayor and his staff filed out onto the stage stark naked and conducted business as usual. *Employment opportunities*, they said. *Crime rates under control.* They talked about everything but the nudity. We watched it on the local station, and the decency censors blurred on and off, confused with all the body parts and what to do with them. The reporters were stunned silent. Their seats were right up close. The mayor and his staffers carried themselves just as they had the day before, but without the wrapping—the grayed suits and ill-fitting dress shirts, gone. Not one of them looked embarrassed or tried to cover themselves up.

This mayor had done a number on us. He was vulgar and rude and only good to people who were exactly like him. We'd thought at first that he was a simple, stupid man. We'd made efforts to unseat him, but he'd outsmarted us, often seemingly by accident. We thought our systems were better equipped to handle a man like him, but in fact they were flimsy and largely untested. There wasn't a scandal or a sound bite our mayor couldn't withstand, couldn't twist in his favor. He'd punished his opponents and gathered enough power to seem untouchable. We'd learned that our town was a scattered, split place—that our beliefs and values were not things we held in common. The whole thing made us scared and disoriented. How had we gotten here? Why had we chosen such a person to lead us?

The mayor announced the nudity decree from behind a glass podium. We saw that he literally flexed his muscles when he figuratively flexed his muscles. He grinned through the whole speech. This stunt was only the latest power play; he wanted to see how far he could push us from who we'd been, before him. Surely this was the final straw. We thought that we would be rid of the mayor, now that everyone could see how small he was.

But the first to disrobe were conservatives. They marched down our streets, naked and loose. They carried signs that asked WHAT'VE YOU GOT TO HIDE?—that proclaimed, LOOK WHAT THE LORD HAS MADE! and MY BODY, MY CHOICE! It was quite a thing to see—droves of bodies, reddening where the sun touched their newly exposed skin. The demonstrators called for us to join them.

We stood in our offices and watched them through the windows. We tightened our ties and pulled at our pencil skirts and didn't know what to make of it.

We'd used nudity against them before. We'd made walls of ourselves and undressed to upset them, and they'd cited us for indecency. Once, we unleashed a row of women on the town hall lawn with letters printed across their bellies like they were football fans. R E S I S T, said the bodies. Printed beneath rows of bare, hanging tits. We called them tits, too. It had upset the supporters then, but the mayor enjoyed it. Our elected official issued a statement the next morning that read, *Sure, I love boobies!* It unsettled us. And now, with this new decree, we feared we'd given him the idea.

It was strange what the nudity did to us—what the nakedness undid.

The mayor's supporters had to follow along or risk admitting that things had gotten out of hand, that in fact they'd been bamboozled in the first place. They filed into banks and churches and sports stadiums, bare and fleshy. They swayed and bellowed in those arenas of worship. The supporters breastfed publicly and learned to make eye contact with one another again. They let their body hair come in thick and full because the mayor had. And were they surprised by how many of their own bodies did not fit the mold—of desirable, acceptable? By how many of their own bodies they had confidently *disallowed*? If so, they didn't mention it to the rest of us. They developed healthy body images to prove a point.

Their children were confused, but resilient, as children are. They questioned their parents, then grew unfazed. Their teenagers were positively burning with the desire to disrobe, though some had already defected and others found rebellion in remaining clothed. We welcomed them to our side with open (sleeved) arms, but the teens rejected us and chose one another. They built their own community on the outskirts of town, and whether they wore clothes or not—whether they went to school, or ate healthy, balanced meals—remained largely unknown.

The rest of us wore layers. We covered up with baggy jeans and sweatshirts. We hid our outlines in defiance of the mayor and everything he stood for. That first winter, we were at a clear advantage. Supporters could only wear shoes, carried umbrellas when it snowed. They sprinted from place to place, or stayed indoors. They talked about moving to Florida.

But the black smog from the local petroleum refinery—in which the mayor had a large investment—climbed into the sky and parted the clouds to let the sun through hot and early that spring. We suffered in the hot seasons, sweltering under our political statements. We carried water to keep hydrated. At public swimming pools and lakes, we watched our opposition splash and frolic. From inside our fabric tents, we squinted through the glare of the sun bouncing off every part of them. We thought that they looked free.

You might guess that sex happened all the time, but it didn't. It probably happened less. Something about the naked body being readily available, so out in the open, made it less desirable. You'd see bodies crammed into bus seats, bodies slouching through produce aisles, bodies exposed to harsh and unflattering lighting. All that flesh laid bare in every kind of setting made it look almost natural. The places, not the people, began to look strange.

Porn habits faltered and dimmed. Gone was the need to click through videos in dark rooms, feeling guilty and depraved. One needed only to go outside and join the world. The sex appeal that emerged was more honest. Lacy underthings were trappings of the past. We stopped asking for nudes, stopped receiving those that were unsolicited in the first place.

We noticed that some of the women who supported the mayor went missing on a regular basis—in groups, or one by one. *Sinister*, we called the pattern, at first. We considered launching an investigation. Though the mayor claimed to love women, he also clearly hated them. But when the missing supporters re-emerged, they seemed unharmed. We learned—painstakingly, in whispers—that they self-elected to remain indoors during their *monthlies*. They were permitted to wear underwear and pads for a week each month as long as they stayed out of sight. While we did not believe menstruation to be unclean, it was reported that more than one woman of the resistance caught herself wishing for a dark room and isolation—for snacks and rest and unfettered time to bleed alone, in peace.

In an act of what we believed to be accidental anticapitalism, the mayor shut down half the town's retail. Clothing stores put everything on sale, then liquidated. The night before Black Friday, supporters burned down the outlet malls. Firefighters arrived sporting hoses and nothing more; they cowered away from the heat, refused to tame the blaze. Though the arsonists stood in full view nearby, keeping warm against the chilly night air, they were not prosecuted.

Instead, the remaining resistance was strip-searched and left bare. Our houses were raided, clothing criminalized. Neighbors reported neighbors when they saw them through windows, still brazen and covered in the safety of their homes.

In the wake of such force, we relented. We had only ever developed a defensive strategy, incorrectly assumed the others would concede with time. Resistance was tiring, and it was hard on us to feel singled out and strange. To feel powerless. We were so hot in our layers that when they were stripped away from us, we mostly felt relief. Those required to cover up by faith or culture experienced shame, but our town was learning to cope with that emotion differently, or to ignore it altogether. Perhaps we were building something new. The mayor felt no shame, and he seemed happy. We hoped to be happy, too.

The nudity was hardly an inconvenience. It took us no time to get ready in the morning—we stepped right from our showers and out the door, climbed into our cars to spend the day filing the same reports that we had filed the week before. And we belonged.

The mayor appeared on television to gloat. He was not a humble man. He strutted to the podium, grinning and posturing. He used our tax dollars to golf daily, and we saw that his tan was evening out. He shushed the constituents gathered before him with a finger to his lips—smiling or sneering behind his upheld pointer. We leaned in. Surely this was the last he would ask of us. The final impossible length. The glow of the TV screens bounced off our pure, naked skin, and we waited for him to tell us we were beautiful.

CHOOSE BLISS

WHEN HER RECKONING BEGINS, CHARLOTTE is meditating toward contentment. She has converted her study into a Relaxation Room, is sitting cross-legged atop a pillow designed for the floor. She hums a flat note. Thinks, *Empty your mind's well, Charlotte. Find your deepest heart.* She imagines her consciousness cracking open like an egg, like a lotus flower, like a fist unclenched in sleep. She resists the urge to scratch the dry skin at her shins. Charlotte looks for peace in the edges of her being, for calm in the depths of her sacrum. When she cannot recall where her sacrum is located, she cracks one eye open and then the other.

Charlotte leans over to flip through her dog-eared copy of *Profound Meditation: Accessing Absolute Intuition*. Initially, she read the book slowly, practicing the techniques bit by bit as they were explained. When that yielded no answers—only sessions spent trying to keep count of her breaths despite the twitch and fidget of her left eyelid and the incessant *kiyahh* of a bird outside her window—she concluded that there was ultimate knowing in the book's conclusion. Fulfillment was a destination, rather than a path. She skipped ahead.

She opens to chapter 8: "Unlocking the Wisdom of Past & Concurrent Selves." She was skeptical at first that such a concept should come so early—only midway through the book—but it's her favorite section now. The book's spine is creased and primed so that it flops to the correct page of its own accord, waiting. Charlotte likes the idea that she is not only herself—that she is an infinite stretch into the past and future, that she has been before and will be again. When she is lonely—which is often, lately—this idea comforts her.

Charlotte spends hours away from her phone, in the Relaxation Room or elsewhere, living the day mindfully—taking walks, folding the laundry precisely, savoring each sip of hibiscus herbal tea as it glides over her tongue. These days she returns to her phone, presses it awake, and more often than not finds nothing waiting. Before, her life seemed filled with a series of crises and tiny disasters that those around her were incapable of solving on their own. Gina's lost the dog again and needs someone to drive her around the neighborhood; Charlotte's mother is caught in a phone scam, her savings vulnerable to an IRS imposter. But now, the world turns even without Charlotte's attention. All is quiet, perhaps due to her newfound positivity.

At the office, Charlotte senses her coworkers do not value her new path. When she speaks to them, their eyes seem eager to buckle and roll in their sockets. Charlotte wishes them sincerity.

She does not think about Richard, and so he fades to the background. Since their separation, her mother treats her differently—

more carefully, like a fractured thing that might shatter with the slightest shift in pressure. When Charlotte described her burgeoning spiritual journey, her mother answered only, *You do whatever you need to, dear.* Charlotte suspects that her mother—a romantic at heart—still hopes that each young man who collects her banking PIN over the phone has her best interest at heart, maintains this hope despite the credit cards she must cancel each time she discovers they don't. Charlotte wishes her truth and clarity.

Charlotte does not think about Richard. She radiates the warmth of her intentions outward and hopes that those around her might one day reflect it back. But she is not entirely sure it reaches them, that they can feel her glow at all. In these times of doubt, she turns again to chapter 8. *You are full,* it assures her. *You are a universe unto yourself. There are multitudes beneath your skin.*

In the Relaxation Room, Charlotte adjusts her posture, realigns her chakras toward her third eye, which rests just beneath the permanent furrow between her brows—a spot that the old Charlotte might have stretched and plumped with lotions, but that now serves as the locus for her innermost attention. On most mornings, she finds the chatter of her thoughts distracting. On most mornings, the aromatic twigs she burns, which smell of forests or concepts like Serenity, make Charlotte sneeze. But this particular morning, her thoughts are low enough that she can lay the ocean sound of her breath over them. She sucks in air and life, breathes out gratitude.

She scans her body and relishes each piece. Her ass is not an ass but a seat, a solid anchor grounding her to the good and steady earth. Her belly—soft and stacked over itself—is a center of emotional digestion. Her uneven breasts are life-giving, untested but full of potential. Charlotte unclenches her jaw. Her beautiful body tingles, and the blood within courses through her. It says, *You are alive. How wonderful it is to be!*

After months of failure and boredom, finally this reward. A high unlike the last one she'd experienced, induced by marijuana, which she hadn't wanted to try, really; which she'd feared would turn on her until her fear pushed it to; which drove her to hide in a closet while Richard and their party guests laughed at her and plowed through the snacks she'd set out for them. A high unlike orgasm, too, which she partially blames for the dissolution of her marriage, because she had trained her body to reach it without her husband until his presence became an impediment. This height most like the steel string of an instrument once plucked, thrumming at a sublime frequency. Finally, this peace. Breath in, breath out. Her body a perfect machine.

"Ahem."

The sound thwacks Charlotte between the eyes, right over her third. Deepest peace trickles away. She chases it, but the room around her begins to reassert itself—the singed-tree smell and the soft buzz of the humidifier, turning distilled water to mist. The old frustration floods back. Her ass is an ass again, her belly—doughy and creased.

"Hello?" a male voice says.

She could not have left the door unlocked. Charlotte is very careful about this sort of thing. Overcautious, even. She does not have a security system, but there is a sign—bought online and staked dead center in the lawn so you can't miss it—warning potential burglars and rapists and killers that she does. Charlotte is frightened by the voice's intrusion now and, if she's being honest, a little thrilled. She has not felt a rush of adrenaline in some time, savors it before inner focus fully leaves her.

Charlotte hears the dull rhythm of fingers tapping the hardwood floor and decides she'd better get it over with. Death, apparently, is an impatient master and not a calm and all-knowing peace as outlined in chapter 15. She takes a final, deep breath, then throws her eyes wide open—intent to take in every detail of her last moments—and looks at and slightly through the first incarnation.

"I thought you might've fallen asleep." He points to the book beside her with a jut of his translucent chin. "I hope you don't actually believe in that crock."

WHEN THE STUDENT IS READY, THE TEACHER
WILL APPEAR.

The man is thin and tall, dressed in a khaki suit gone baggy around the knees. He has the look of a professor—a spindly and hollow academic posture.

Charlotte gathers his details slowly. She sees him as though through a thin layer, like gauze or wrinkled Saran Wrap. Each time she looks away and back again or blinks, the ripples between them have shifted slightly and behind them the figure is changed, barely. A new part exposed, another hazy.

"Are you a ghost?" she asks.

"Am I a ghost," he answers. From the way he says it, in a too-high imitation of her voice, she knows that he means, *No*.

"What, then?"

"I am myself. And you, I suppose."

"Are you a hallucination?"

"Of sorts," he says.

She feels that this presence is toying with her. The gray wisps of hair across his pate—now shiny, now dull—are spun and bushy to cover what he's lost. He smells strongly—almost unbearably—of cigarettes. It cuts through the other scents in the air. Charlotte feels the edges of a headache and begins to breathe through her mouth.

"Are you here to tell me something?" she says.

"What did you have in mind?"

Charlotte falters. "The book says . . . I don't know—wisdom? Or a truth. Some sort of deeper awakening?"

"Do you think you could provide an example?" he says, sneering now.

Charlotte flips the guide open again, scans the page before her. *You are everything you need, and everyone,* it says. *No one deserves to be here more than you.* Perhaps this is a test.

"Maybe there's a riddle. Something I need to unlock first?"

"A riddle," he says, considering. He looks up, or maybe to the left. The shine of his eyes is difficult to track.

"What is willing and ripe and ready to learn?" He grins madly once it's out, a Cheshire expression with dull and yellowed teeth.

Fruit, she thinks. *Or. No. The mind? Or me. Is the answer me?* She does not guess aloud, partially because she is puzzling through it and partially as a test of her own, to see if this apparition is truly *of* her. If it can read her thoughts.

"Nothing?" he asks, crouched down at her level. He perches on the ball mounds of his feet, surprisingly nimble. She expects to hear his knees crack, but hears nothing. "You're stumped, then?"

Charlotte shrugs.

"I'll tell you the answer," he says. "To this question and to all of life's questions."

Charlotte leans forward, hoping for the secret of the universe to reveal itself. But knowing, also, that it cannot come like this.

"An undergraduate," he says, already cackling.

The pain in Charlotte's head goes *tharum tharum tharum*.

WE MUST EXPLORE THE DARKNESS OF OUR PAST TO
ILLUMINATE OUR PRESENT.

The professor is not a manifestation of divine truth. He is an asshole.

He dismisses Charlotte's questions with a mean and nearly predatory brand of deflection.

"Where have you come from?" she asks.

He says, "Of course you're here alone."

"Why me?" she asks.

"There's nowhere else I'd rather be."

Why this *vision?* she wonders. Why has her mind's eye summoned such a presence? The professor is unfamiliar, unpleasant— perhaps the result of a prolonged trance she simply cannot snap out of. Charlotte honors her powers of concentration. *Thank you*, she tells herself. *Enough now.*

But the professor does not fade. He is still actualized in the Relaxation Room. Charlotte feels that he can see too much of her. She takes a folded blanket from the floor beside her, throws it over her bare shoulders like a shawl. This does not help and soon she is even more uncomfortable: it's June and the room is humidified.

The professor picks up items, examines them, puts them down in different places. The small gong and mallet, now separated. A Himalayan salt lamp—bought on sale from Home Depot, though Charlotte would've paid full price—now turned to reveal the cord. The professor lifts a handful of seashells from a vase, lets them sift through slim fingers. Charlotte forgets her headache. Her nose, fatigued by everything in the room, has stopped registering any scent at all. The professor worries a rosary, a remnant of when she and Richard were still Catholic. He lifts the hunk of rose quartz from the floor, exposing the gash in the hardwood it covers.

"Do you have a particular belief set," he asks, "or just everyone else's?" He drops the crystal, lets it gouge the varnish again.

"Namaste," she tries. Charlotte stands with her two big toes pressed together, with her heels slightly apart. She closes her eyes, makes her hands a prayer shape and raises that steeple to her forehead. She bows from the waist, back straight. She rises and opens her eyes just the tiniest bit, but he is still with her.

"Case in point," says the professor.

"The divine light in me honors the divine light in you."

"Jesus."

She pushes the blanket off her shoulders, bends down to retrieve her handbook. She rifles through the table of contents— "Acknowledging the Oversoul, The Clairaudient Multiverse"—but finds nothing about closing off connection to the self. Perhaps wires have gotten crossed. The professor might have answered the wrong call, maybe does not belong here at all.

"You're sure there's not something you want from me?" she says.

He Cheshire-grins again. "I never said *that.*" She's pretty sure he winks.

Charlotte decides to lose him. Surely the cure for a placid mind is the world's chatter. She slides into her sandals and heads out the front door. She blinks wildly for a moment in the threshold. The sun is high and bright; it's later than she would've guessed, already afternoon. Charlotte wills herself to engage with these surroundings—this neighborhood—in a way she rarely does. They'd moved here to shorten Richard's commute only three years before. She doesn't know her neighbors and feels too much time has passed to try. She is more familiar with their dogs: the hateful Chihuahua next door; the German shepherd two streets over that she finds handsome; a stunted poodle breed that paces circles in its yard.

Charlotte walks, trying to take in everything around her. She notes the flowers pushing through landscaping, the sacred geometry of the petals. Charlotte studies the imperfections in the road's asphalt. She counts the cars parked along the curb, peeks through windows and into back seats. She stops to watch some neighborhood boys playing basketball in the cul-de-sac. How earnestly they shoulder one another aside, seize upon the fouls committed against them. How fragile their knees look beneath loose and shiny shorts, all a size too big. The hoop tilts precariously each time they shoot, then rights itself.

But the professor is there, there, there. His features are even hazier in the daylight, but he follows beside her or behind her, stops to observe when she does.

"I never understood the appeal of athletics," he says, watching the boys too. "So masculine. So *philistine*."

One of the boys rolls an ankle and sinks to the pavement. The others crowd around him, and Charlotte looks around for other witnesses—a chaperone, a parent. Seeing none, she pivots, catches the glint of the professor's raised brow in her peripherals. Surely, there are mothers with ice packs and elastic bandages, waiting just inside the house. Charlotte walks away with the professor still trailing her, hears the fallen boy or one of his friends say *Fuck*.

Charlotte speeds up. She is sweating, but the professor keeps pace. She is not wearing the right bra for jogging, and also, she does not jog.

"Allergy season," he says.

Charlotte steps beyond the arc of a neighbor's sprinkler. She waves to the deliveryman, who barely notices.

"What time is it?" says the professor.

She picks some stalks of forsythia to carry home.

"All the bees are dying."

Charlotte returns home and thinks, too late, to slam the door behind her. The professor follows her in, stands out of the door's path.

"I *do* have some things to do today," she tells him, but she doesn't really and he knows it.

"By all means," he says. He scoops up the copy of *Profound Meditation*, settles into the only chair in the room, which hangs from the ceiling like a wicker cocoon. The professor nestles in among the cushions. He leaves one foot planted on the floor, drapes the other ankle over his knee. He lets the book fall open to the middle. The chair does not spin as it does when she sits in it.

Before calling professionals, Charlotte had intended to install the chair herself. She hoped to be the kind of woman who wouldn't shy from DIY. She watched several instructional videos where people—mostly men—made the whole task seem manageable. In one, a woman plonked into her self-hung hammock, radiating satisfaction until the beam above her cracked, dropping her and chunks of plaster and pink insulation fluff onto the floor. The video cut to static after, and Charlotte still wonders, sometimes, who posted it.

The handymen who installed the chair drilled holes into the ceiling, fixed sturdy-looking rungs into an imperceptible skeleton of crossbeams. When Charlotte dropped in to check their progress, the men were shucking each other across the back, laughing.

"Pardon us, ma'am," the thicker one said when he saw her. Their facial hair made it hard to tell their ages, hard to say if she should feel threatened by the men or maternal. The pair straightened up and continued the job more soberly. They nodded their thanks as she deposited bottles of water in the doorway and backed out of the room.

When they'd finished and were on their way out, the same one—the talker, maybe the boss—said, "Sorry about earlier." He explained that the last time they'd done an installation like hers, it was for a tattooed couple's sex swing. He assured Charlotte that they didn't think of her that way, knew she wasn't that type.

He'd winked at her then. Charlotte felt that, somehow, men were always winking at her for the wrong reasons. Before the implication of what he'd said had fully settled, Charlotte replied, "Oh, thank you," smiled, and shut the door.

> YOU ARE A RADICAL SOURCE OF LOVE. ACCEPT ALL
> PARTS OF YOUR BEING TO HARNESS YOUR
> EVOLUTIONARY POTENTIAL.

The professor is ubiquitous. He tours the house, sticks a finger into the soil of each of her houseplants. He opens closets and peeks inside, leaves the doors standing wide open.

He follows her to the bathroom. Charlotte is unaware of this, at first. Just as she has decided that she's alone and has settled onto the toilet, a voice behind her says, "Trust me—I don't want to be here either," and it startles the pee loose. He leans against the tank, averting his gaze, and Charlotte worries about the sound of her stream as it strikes the porcelain bowl. She avoids his eye in the mirror while she washes her hands.

He follows her to the kitchen afterward. He rifles through the contents of her fridge, her pantry.

"What the hell is this?" he says, retrieving a jar from a back shelf. The liquid inside is amber and thin, topped by a jellyfish cap of slick and viscous culture.

"A scoby," she tells him, "for kombucha." She says this as if everyone might have such a thing in their pantry, beside the bags of rice and sugar. In truth, she's been neglecting the yeasty hull, ignoring it on the pantry shelf so long that a new fungal layer has grown beneath the first. There are a number of jams and sauces and pickling things set on the shelves—produced in a sort of rustic frenzy—that she's too afraid to try. The concept of letting things ferment—spoil just enough—makes her stomach turn.

Her phone lights up on the counter. It's set to silent so that she can find peace, but also so that calls go straight to voicemail. She recorded the outgoing message five weeks ago, just after Richard left. It's simple—*I'll get back to you as soon as time is willing. Be well.* When she played it back, the smooth tone of her voice was a sound she hardly recognized. She liked this version of herself. This calm, sure version. Now, she unlocks the phone with her thumbprint, and there is a missed call from Richard. A missed call and a voicemail from Richard.

"Wonder what that's about," the professor says at her shoulder.

Charlotte closes out of the voicemail inbox, switches tactics. "You'll be bored by this, I'm afraid." She picks up her bill from the wireless company, dials the number listed. She presses 1 for English, 4 for an issue concerning her plan, 2 to register dissatisfaction, 9 to speak to a representative. The human option is always buried.

"They've put me on hold," she says, covering the speaker with her fingertips. But the professor lingers beside her. She settles on the floor and he sits beside her, too close, trying to bring his ear close to the receiver. He keeps just enough space between them so as not to touch her. They sit like this while a jazzy pan-flute melody plays on a loop. When the teenage voice picks up on the other end to collect her name and reason for calling, it is already bored.

Charlotte tries to cancel her service. "I don't use the internet at the house anymore," she says. "I don't like to be so plugged in."

"What?" says the voice. Sort of rudely. Weren't they supposed to be polite?

"If I need to use the internet, I go elsewhere," she explains. "This house is connected to something higher." She chuckles for the voice's benefit. "I have no need for Wi-Fi."

The voice says that she is under contract. It says that she is renting a device from them, that uninstalling it would require her to pay a steep fee. The voice says it's cheaper for her to simply stay on the plan.

"How is that possible?" she says, but the voice starts calculating sums and it loses her.

Here, the professor comes in handy. He listens closely to the calculations, shakes his head. He feeds her things to say and because she is losing, anyway, Charlotte repeats them into the phone. She corrects the voice's math. She calls this criminal. She replaces the professor's *haji* with *son* because the voice is just a young man trying to do his job for a company that exploits him to accomplish its greedy ends. And anyway, the only accent she detects is slightly midwestern. The professor's racism is freewheeling and inaccurate. She asks to speak to the young man's manager. When the manager is unavailable, the professor says, she says, "A supervisor, then." The boy begins to stutter. She raises her voice. She says, "Where are you located? I'd be happy to come and speak to you in person." The boy sighs. He says, "Okay, here's what I can do," and he offers her a deal and she takes it because it still feels like winning.

She hangs up and the professor says, "Well done."

It seems that they have settled on harmony.

> PERFECTION IS ILLUSORY. FACETS OF THE SELF ARE
> NOT IDEAL OR INCORRECT. THEY SIMPLY ARE.

Charlotte cooks pasta while the professor fiddles with a television, tries to get it working. She's fished it from the back of the closet—a small flat-screen that once sat on the kitchen counter, distracting her even there. She has consented to let the professor set it up in the corner of the empty living room. Charlotte lifts a goddess statue whose name she cannot recall—with stretched lobes and stone detailing carved to look like necklace beads— from the table by the ears. She puts it in the Relaxation Room, where it maybe should've been all along. She hands the professor the remote and leaves it to him to program the cable they've just gotten an excellent deal on. She can cancel it when he leaves her.

While she boils noodles and pours the contents of a sauce jar—store-bought—into a pot, the professor shouts comments and questions she must exit the kitchen repeatedly to hear.

"What?" she asks, coming into the room.

"Are you sure we've got all the right extensions here?"

Charlotte shrugs, turns back. She slices up olives to add to the sauce, fishes capers out of a narrow jar with fork tines.

"Will dinner be ready soon?" he says.

"You remind me of my husband," Charlotte says. Sometimes she thought Richard was driving her crazy on purpose. She can see now that they were not a well-matched pair, that their souls were misaligned and dissonant. But back then, she had taken things so personally. *My god, Richard,* she might've said. *If you have a question, come back into the goddamn room and ask it. I'm not going to chase you around this house.* Their whole marriage had been like that: two people trying to hear each other, standing in different rooms.

Charlotte spoons servings onto two plates, carries them to the professor. He's in a sour mood. He has turned the TV to face the wall, and a blue, blank light bounces off the paint.

"Let's just go back in there," he says, heading for the Relaxation Room.

They sit on the floor, and the professor doesn't touch his plate. Charlotte sucks up her noodles self-consciously, with a palm hovering over her mouth. They play a game of cards after dinner but cannot agree on the rules. She says, *Rummy* and he says, *Gin rummy,* and they see that they've not been playing the game the same way at all.

"Well, let's get to it," he says, laying his hand down. It's stronger than hers. "I bet you'd like to know how I died."

The professor is a past life, then—his energy recast for another. Charlotte raises an eyebrow but keeps her gaze on the cards in her hands. She collects his, shuffles. She tents the deck with her fingers to make a bridge. The professor tells her details of his life that seem unrelated to his death. His area of study, publications. The name of his tenured chair and the jealousy of his colleagues. The squander of his talents at an obscure university, how he's glad it's ended now.

"But how, exactly?" she says.

"I was sleeping with a student. My heart went out." He seems proud of this. She thinks his eyes are twinkling.

But Charlotte imagines the scene differently. The unfortunate girl, hating herself for the sacrifices she's willing to make for a competitive GPA. She has a law school application to consider, after all. Parts of the professor are attractive in a stately way, but his hands are thin and slightly spotted and the girl does not like to see them cupped around her breasts. His lower half is obscured by the sheets as he thrusts, and she prefers it this way. And then, the girl as Charlotte sees her, relieved when the gray wisp of a man atop her bulges his eyes and collapses, lies still. For a time, she must think this is part of the show. A dramatic finish. When the girl does not hear him gasping and they have been close for too long, she will put her hands on his shoulders, press up. He's gone completely limp, and she will scream and flail free, will call the police and leave before they arrive. The girl will return to her dorm room and tell no one, will crawl into her sheets and cry. She will never truly learn to enjoy sex. She will remember the moment for the rest of her life, and especially when anyone uses the term *dead weight*.

Charlotte focuses on the professor again, whose smile has faded. The haughty set to his chin is back, but it is harder to believe. He looks angry. He looks fragile, even hurt. Can he read Charlotte's thoughts after all? The professor's outline flickers, then dissolves before her.

> KARMIC TIES AND CORDS OF ATTACHMENT MUST BE
> TENDED TO. A FRAYED ROPE SNAPS WHEN TESTED.

Charlotte is alone again. She closes her eyes in gratitude, snaps them back open to be sure. There is only the static buzz from the television in the other room. Charlotte stands and switches it off. She leaves their dishes in the sink, scoops up her phone from the counter. Two more missed calls now, both from Richard. The voicemail. No professor in the kitchen, no professor in the bedroom. She climbs into the covers and unlocks the screen. She calls Richard back.

He picks up after three rings. "Hello?"

"It's Charlotte," she says, though he must know.

"Did you get my message?" She listens for a change in his voice, perhaps a brooding note. Richard is not the kind of man to admit fault outright. Of all that Charlotte has attuned herself toward, she is perhaps best suited to hear what her husband doesn't say when he should. "I need that club," he says.

Charlotte holds her breath.

"The five iron?" he continues. "I think it must've fallen outta my golf bag. Check the garage, will y—"

Charlotte hangs up. Solitude is a gift. She repeats the line over and over again in her head, and she must fall asleep because then, she is waking up to a weight in the bed beside her and that sharp tobacco scent. She worries about it seeping into the sheets. How much of this is lasting? How much of it is real?

"Where's your husband?" asks the professor. In the dark, the question is almost soft.

"Away," she says.

"Where?"

Charlotte does not answer. She is not completely sure.

"Do you miss him?" says the professor—deep down, a man who hopes he is missed.

"Sometimes." Charlotte does not want the professor to think there is a role to fill, but she cannot help herself. "We were so young when it started." And then, "He used to call me Charlatan. It was part of his pickup line, actually. Not particularly romantic or sweet, when I think about it now, but I'd spent nineteen years with my name, and no one'd ever thought to call me anything else. It worked, among other things. We married quickly. Called it a whirlwind romance."

The professor is quiet. His breathing is steady, and she cannot tell if he has fallen asleep.

"He called me that the whole way through," she says. "But it changed, went mean. It wasn't funny anymore. When we had company over, it felt like he was spitting it at me. He used it in front of my mother." Her voice cracks, just barely, and she hopes that the professor will not reach out to comfort her.

"You should always be Charlotte," he says instead. He does not touch her at all.

In the morning he is gone, and her pillow smells of fabric softener and dust.

SHAME AND REGRET ARE FUNDAMENTALLY RESTRICTIVE
EMOTIONS. CHOOSE BLISS.

Charlotte finds the beetle in the Relaxation Room. She's gone there to meditate before she leaves for work. She's gone there to check for the professor, and she spots the bug crawling across the cushion of the hanging chair. She nearly sits on it. The insect is no bigger than her pinkie fingernail, and Charlotte leans in to study the pattern across its back. It is tribal and geometric, shaped like a warrior's shield.

She raises her finger above the insect, poised to crush or flick it away. Instead, she brings the finger down to rest on its back. She is gentle. She uses only enough pressure to pin it there, to make a tiny halo of indentation in the cushion. She holds the creature there, homes in on the feeling of it beneath her fingertip. She tries to determine whether or not she can feel its pulse, or the motion of its tiny legs scrambling to find purchase and carry it to safety. But the insect radiates calm. Its shell is firm but fragile. It holds the tension of an uncracked knuckle.

When she lifts her finger, the beetle does not move. Charlotte is worried she's killed it, shocked its tiny heart beyond what it can bear. She prods the back of the insect—perhaps the thorax or its abdomen—and it moves. It does not scurry away from her, but rotates to face the threat of her finger—a giant to it, proportion-ally. Its mouthparts twitch and taste the air. Such an act of bravery moves her. It feels, just then, like a sign.

Charlotte scoots closer and crouches down. She gets level with the insect, until their eyes are even—her two and its many—both taking in all they can of the other. Charlotte sees herself the way Richard might, if he were to come looking for her or the golf club. The way her mother might, or Gina: Charlotte crouched and speaking to a chair. No, a bug on the seat of a chair. Charlotte believes despite this. She sees herself as the beetle must see her: as vast. She so wants to be infinite, rather than flawed.

"Are you here for me?" she asks the insect.

Its antennae wriggle intently, which she takes to mean, *I am.*

SUCH GREAT HEIGHT
AND CONSEQUENCE

TO BE CLEAR, THE STATUE came down for its own protection. Not because the lawmakers and politicians and folks at city hall finally grew themselves a conscience. Not because they wanted a new chapter for Aberdeen, a new image of unity and tolerance, though that's what they might say now. To be clear, enough people had left the safety and comfort of their own homes to march around the statue of General James Hixby and enough of them were circling it, leering up at the statue like they had never noticed it before and hoisting their handmade signs in its direction—almost threateningly, as if the general could read them—while enough camera crews had arrived on the scene to film the protest and label the town and its statue as *backward* and *bigoted* and then some little shithead snuck up to the statue under the cover of night and proclaimed in shining letters that *The general sucked his horse's DICK!*,[1] that someone up top gave the order for the statue to be removed and stored somewhere *more suitable*.

---

[1] There exists no historical evidence to confirm this claim.

Plenty of folks wrote in to suggest more appropriate locations for the general—some of them sincerely—but where he sits now is probably a storage locker in some undisclosed facility. The statue was removed in the middle of the night, at a date and time undisclosed to the public.[2] What they left in its wake was the pedestal.

All accounts suggest that James Hixby—called Jim by his familiars, as well as, reportedly, "The Confederacy's Thunderbolt"[3]—was a real son of a bitch. He came from money and was born with both a silver spoon in his mouth as well as a slave he inherited upon birth whose job it was to polish said silver spoon. The Hixby plantation, built on land that today hosts the Aberdeen Wildlife Park, maintained a relatively small group of slaves,[4] who were said to be treated well by the family.[5] Though the Hixby home remains intact as a historical structure on the park's grounds, it was discovered during renovations to expand the Big Cat Pavilion that the exhibit had been built right over top of slave burial grounds, determined to be such by the nicks and breaks and general signs of torment evident on the unearthed bones. The remains of the slaves were reinterred on a plot just behind the big house they once served, with a small plaque to explicate the historical

---

2 This has since come to be viewed as a missed PR opportunity.

3 Though this was asserted as fact by a genuine Daughter of the Confederacy at the original unveiling ceremony, no historical record confirms the nickname.

4 Roughly thirty to forty-five owned individuals.

5 There is much debate over what benevolent slaveholding entails.

context.[6] The Big Cat Pavilion, now expanded, features a pair of lethargic mountain lions named Pat and Christopher Walken.

It is said that James Hixby's dying request—as he was suffering from a lethal infection caused by a poorly dressed knife wound to his abdomen—was to bequeath all his worldly possessions and inheritance to his horse, Whicket, the very steed he'd been memorialized riding into battle.[7] It's widely held that General James Hixby sustained the inciting wound far from the battlefield.[8] The statue portrayed the general waving a bayonet ahead of him and looking back over his shoulder, as if he were cheering his battalion onward. Whicket is shown rearing and chomping at the bit. The statue was erected in 1905, forty years after the Confederacy had turned tail and scampered off. Until its removal, small Confederate flags could still be seen tucked into the general's curled fist some Sunday mornings in tribute, before the caretaker arrived to remove them.

Popular opinion held that the empty pedestal left in the general and Whicket's wake was unsightly. Some said it served as an unwelcome reminder of what had been there before. Others complained that without its topper, the pedestal was just a scarred hunk of concrete, set right in the middle of our town's most idyllic

---

[6] The plaque, which is often overgrown with weeds, reads, "Here lie former servants of the Hixby Family. May they find some comfort here." It does not specify the names of the deceased, as no original grave markers were present or accounted for.

[7] This request was not honored.

[8] Rumor has it that the general was more lover than fighter, at least when it came to other men's wives.

park. It should be mentioned, too, that though the majority of the graffiti scrawled across Whicket's flank and leg was removed along with the statue, some of it had trailed onto the pedestal and despite the caretaker's painstaking efforts to remove it, the paint would not rub off completely. The remainder had been spray-painted in silver so that, though faded, the top of the pedestal still shone gently with the word *DICK*. It practically glittered at dusk.

Some folks suggested that the removal of the statue and the now-empty pedestal was an opportunity. A small coalition of librarians released a statement that read, *We have such a rich history here in Aberdeen. Let us uphold our best and brightest, rather than some racist loser on his poor, innocent horse.* They suggested a list of figures to memorialize in the general's wake—people born and raised in Aberdeen who'd gone on to do bigger things. The inventor of the waffle press had grown up in town. Aberdeen produced a famous '50s-era scat singer, an almost-astronaut, and the man who first rafted the length of the Chattahoochee. Aberdeen was also the birthplace of a raccoon that acted in the original Dr. Doolittle films and had once saved a boy from choking by slapping him squarely in the back.[9] The subject of the replacement monument was to be put up for a vote online, along with a campaign to raise the funds to build it.

But while that was running, the pedestal stood empty, still weathered and gray and disagreeable. In an effort to quell the dissenting opinions that flooded in as to what to do with it in

---

9 This suggestion was later struck, as evidence emerged that the raccoon had severely bitten the boy immediately afterward.

the meantime, the local Parks Department circulated a list. For two hours of any given day, residents could sign up to stand on the empty pedestal and do whatever they pleased, as long as it could not be deemed hateful, harmful, or illegal. Spots would be issued on a first-come, first-served basis. Documentation from the Parks Department's meeting implies that the sign-up sheet was not intended to be taken seriously,[10] though in practice, it was.

The idea was wildly popular, first with supporters of the general and Whicket, then with dissenters of those supporters, and so on. Within two months of the statue's removal, all the steam had died out from that original debate, the way these things often play out. What was left in its stead were folks who truly wanted to stand on a pedestal—to whatever end—and the folks who didn't want to find they had missed out.

Given the political climate, it became uncomfortable for certain people to take their turns on the pedestal. For those who'd always held the power, the raised platform provided a visual representation of where each of them stood on any given day, a step above the rest, regardless of merit. Some relished their time

---

[10] Excerpted from meeting minutes: *Chair proposes that something must be done about the pedestal; suggests community involvement. Chair counters that his inboxes are full of community involvement. Chair suggests that if the people know what's best, then the whole ordeal should be handed over to them. Chair agrees; posits that if the general did such a bad job, why not let the people give it a try? Chair inquires, Well, how long would you give them up there? Chair suggests a couple hours at maximum, lest anyone actually take them up on the offer, fall out in the heat, then cost a fortune in settlements. Chair seconds the motion. Motion approved.*

up there. The park was central, and residents stopped through on lunch breaks, on trips to the grocery store. In the slots on the local news where they'd once played shots of traffic or indistinguishable ankles as they walked across the sidewalk, they now played the feed from the pedestal—a livestream they'd established to deter further defacement—over anchors shuffling their papers and clearing their throats in preparation for the day's report. It was difficult not to notice how many white men seized upon the pedestal's opportunity, difficult to ignore how many of their wives signed up for the next day's slot, equally proud and venomous, though so much of what the wives professed from the height of the pedestal worked against their own interests.

The idea was floated, for a spell, that anyone from an underrepresented community in Aberdeen should have extra time on the pedestal. Practically speaking, though, it became difficult to parse out who qualified for these slots and who didn't and, when pressed, at least one potential candidate sucked her cheeks and said—in short—No, thank you.[11] This caveat was put to rest. Instead, it became a sort of civic duty to take a turn way up on the pedestal.

Folks used their time for a variety of pursuits.

Suzy Pine, to the delight of her parents and classmates, used her time on the pedestal to direct a large game of Red Light, Green Light until the children got too far away to hear her, at which point Suzy Pine began to cry and threw a tantrum that embarrassed her parents and classmates. She was lifted away from the pedestal and carried home, though she could be seen reaching

---

11 The exact response was reportedly more colorful.

over her mother's shoulder as she was hauled away, whining, *But it's not time to go yet!*[12]

Wendy Howard noticed how the light struck the pedestal just so, and, in her allotted time, used the platform to sun. She climbed right up and stepped out of her dress to reveal the bathing suit beneath it, then began to layer on a coconut-scented tanning oil, though that sort of thing had been proven unhealthy and had gone out of style long ago. Wendy laid out her sundress in place of a towel and draped her bikini-clad form across it, turning when she felt herself catching a burn. It was suggested that this violated the terms of the pedestal as it related to public nudity, but because Wendy was not nude and also because she was not visibly uncomfortable in any way, but rather supremely confident in her skin—studying anyone who stopped by to ogle her over the rim of her sunglasses—Wendy was permitted to stay for the duration of her time slot. She was noticeably more tanned by its conclusion.

Hernán Ríos was incredibly shy, but wanted to work on his public speaking, as he was preparing to deliver a speech at his brother's wedding. He pulled the speech from his shirt pocket, then unfolded and proceeded to deliver it, haltingly, with pauses for the laughter he presumed he'd be drawing from the crowd. It was noted that Hernán rushed at times, particularly during the moments in his speech when he complimented his soon-to-be sister-in-law. Each time he reached the end, Hernán smiled and made as if to step down before righting himself and beginning the speech again.

---

[12] Suzy was correct. There was an hour of her slot left.

Jacob Lee had spent his young life learning all he could about trains—their operations and mechanics and track systems throughout the U.S. and abroad—and used the entire duration of his time on the pedestal to talk about them. Who among the townsfolk could say they didn't learn something new that day?

Dr. Hilling, rather than giving a report on public health or proper hygiene, instead used his time to work through a book of crossword puzzles that he'd been given as a gift, but rarely had the time to do. Dr. Hilling used a pen and could be seen scrunching his brow and lifting his gaze in contemplation. When frustrated, he sought help from whichever residents happened to be passing through the park at that particular moment. *What's six letters for a climber's victory?*[13] he asked. *Does anyone know what won the 1994 Tony for best revival?*[14] He did not want passersby to use their phones to search the clues—that was cheating, he said—yet became visibly affected when they could not answer. It's said that at one point, he punched through a page with his ballpoint while trying to write over an answer, then threw both the pen and book of puzzles to the ground below. Dr. Hilling spent the remainder of his time on the pedestal sulking, only to climb down to search in the falling light for the items he'd cast away.[15]

---

[13] SUMMIT.

[14] *CAROUSEL.*

[15] Dr. Hilling denies any reports of poor or sullen conduct and says that he is more than capable of finishing crosswords easily and without assistance. The livestream's recordings are not accessible to the general public in order to verify this claim.

Leslie Adams used his time to explain how Leslie was not *necessarily* a girl's name, and that generations of Leslie Adamses before him had been men who opened factories and businesses and carried the name proudly until they, too, decided to name their firstborn sons Leslie.

Janet Baitling knew far too much about everyone. When folks saw her name on the sign-up sheet, they grew nervous about what she might say. She approached with a portable step-ladder and arranged herself atop the pedestal in a foldout chair, her feet crossed daintily at the ankles. Janet had amassed quite the audience, which was the thing she wanted most. She stayed silent, swelling up with power, for the majority of her time, but as soon as anyone walked away—out of boredom or to make an appointment or to pick up their children from school—Janet told those who remained gathered around her the deepest secret she knew about the one who'd left, which for some was merely an embarrassing thing they'd done in sixth grade, but for others concerned the substantial debt they'd accumulated by ordering antique Hummels over the internet, or talking to a phone sex line operated out of Taos.[16]

E. J. McClain practiced his violin solo with his eyes closed shut, letting the beauty of Chopin's Nocturne in C sharp minor flow through his fingertips and bones and marrow, and out into the surrounding park.

---

[16] An investigation is reportedly ongoing to determine Janet's methods for gathering information, though it's been stalled substantially by rumors that Janet has dirt on the Aberdeen Police Department, too.

A traveling preacher took a turn at the pedestal. It was argued that he was not a true resident, but it was also argued that all of this earth was home to God and therefore unto his shepherds. Folks learned quickly that the preacher's sermon was of a fire and brimstone variety—that he was of the opinion that Aberdeen was chock-full of sinners and burning up. Susan Childers, too sweet for her own good, asked the preacher if he might like a glass of water seeing as how hot it was up there on the pedestal—maybe *that* was what he was sensing, rather than the overwhelming presence of sin? Once she'd gone and fetched it, the preacher took a sip, then called out, *POISON WATER FROM YOUR POISON WELLS* and dumped the rest of the contents right over Susan's head, in a sort of cursed baptism. Susan wept and dismissed herself from the sermon, dripping. Still, some townsfolk remained around the pedestal's perimeter while the preacher carried on, presumably enraptured by his wisdom and fury. Each of them kept a safer distance than Susan had.

Yani Reston wanted to know who among us was interested in becoming our own boss by selling clinically proven and yummy dietary supplements with unbeatable results at a fraction of the prices offered in big-box stores.[17]

Reggie Kent had an upcoming track meet he intended to stay

---

[17] Yani invited those around the pedestal to a taste-testing to be held at her residence the following Saturday afternoon. Those in attendance were required to sign a waiver before testing said tastes and went home with salted-caramel- and banana-flavored samples, whose packaging read in bold letters, *Not regulated by the FDA.*

fit for, and used his time on the pedestal to complete a workout composed of squats and over-unders and ab exercises, which some folks saw as a fitness class in the park—the sort of public entertainment usually offered only in towns or cities much larger than theirs. Eventually, Reggie began to give cues to the impromptu audience spread out before him on yoga mats and blankets. *Twenty flutter kicks—let's go!* he called out, and while many attendees were appreciative of a free class, a few shouted back, *Count louder!* or, *This beginner's class is way too hard!*

The fourth-grade class of Aberdeen Elementary used the pedestal as a makeshift stage for their spelling bee. They had originally reserved the school's auditorium for the event, but it was double-booked over a dance recital. A set of stairs was wheeled up and secured to the pedestal, and parents set out lawn chairs to cheer on the contestants. Though *clandestine* and *antebellum*— among other words—were spelled successfully, *saltine* was the final word of the contest, as the runner-up confused the placement of vowels.[18] The runner-up was gracious about the loss, though his parents were not.

Stella Rainsom, a young activist and budding historian, announced all the slaveholding families of Aberdeen and the surrounding counties, which was an admittedly lengthy list, from the pedestal. She then listed the names and ages of their slaves at date of purchase, sale, or death,[19] which was an even lengthier list.

---

[18] S-A-L-T-E-N-I.

[19] In cases where this data was available.

Charlotte Denning had not slept much the night before and was very tired. She set up a sunshade and donned a sleep mask and curled up on the pedestal to take a nap. Though the shade protected her from public view, it is assumed that Charlotte slept soundly. She dismounted looking refreshed.

Parker Lee Woodard proposed to his girlfriend from the height of the pedestal, which she both anticipated[20] and tearily accepted.

Wylie Lennox brought his dog onto the pedestal, a rescued Rottweiler mix, who, despite the fact that he was a good, sweet boy and lacked an aggressive bone in his thick, muscular body, could not catch a pat or a *here-boy!* from the residents of Aberdeen on his twice-daily walks. Wylie had named the dog HamBone in an effort to placate his neighbors, though in practice, this worked against his interests by making the dog sound ravenous. While he hoped that their time atop the pedestal would soften the dog's public image—*See how he can sit, lie down, roll over? HamBone, give me a paw!*—both had to leave the pedestal before their allotted time was out because Wylie had forgotten a water dish and HamBone was a black-coated dog on a concrete platform in the dead of summer.

Faye, the longtime waitress at the diner, who did not write her last name on the sign-up sheet, but who was so well known about town that she did not need to include it, used her time—not to cheerily comment on how cute everyone's toddlers were or how

---

20 She had mentioned the phrase *oval cut* in conversation. Shortly thereafter, she had walked Parker to the jewelry store and shown him the very ring she wanted. Two weeks before his slot on the pedestal, Parker had asked for her ring size.

excited she was about their daughters' graduations, the way she did while taking their orders—but instead to pontificate about their poor table manners. Faye knew who among the townspeople could be expected to chew with their mouths wide open or to forget their to-go boxes on the table or to tear their napkins up into little bits that then mixed with the syrup left pooled beneath their plates when the table was cleared. She had opinions on the tip you owed a server after your child, who had no business at a restaurant if she couldn't act right, had crushed and then dropped each strawberry sliver and berry from their fruit cup onto the tiled floor beneath the booth. Faye said that if one more person held up their glass without looking at her, and then swirled the ice around to signal for a refill, so help her God. She said that the only way for her to retrieve that extra lemon wedge for you was with her fingers, because the diner always misplaced the designated set of tongs. Do with that knowledge what you will, said Faye, and plenty else, before climbing down for her shift.

It seemed that, given the opportunity and platform to do so, most of Aberdeen had something to say or do or play or confess. There had not been an outlet or attraction quite like the pedestal in some time, and it was generally held that the platform was a productive means of expression and community-building. Yes, some got up on the pedestal and grew shy, then climbed right back down. Others had to be reminded when their time was up, and at least one resident was forcefully removed.[21] But generally, the pedestal maintained its own sense of order.

---

[21] By residents, not by authorities.

Over time, it became increasingly clear that the pedestal was not holding up well to its new purpose. It seemed that *set in stone* held true for sediment, too, and that after decades beneath an inert cad of a soldier and his trusty steed, the new task of holding up an entire town, even one by one, proved wearing. Wendy Howard had dripped tanning oil onto the platform, which the stone had soaked right up. One resident, who'd signed up for a slot under the pseudonym *The Wolf*, strung a series of extension cords from the back of a nearby ice-cream shop where he reportedly worked and hefted an amp and electric guitar onto the platform. When, midperformance, his audience began to disperse, The Wolf grew enraged and hacked his guitar against the pedestal repeatedly, which, besides destroying the instrument, chipped one edge of the platform and littered the base with flecks of glittering, orange enamel. The pedestal had grown dingy from all the shoes that tracked across it and pocked where residents' grills and golf swings and easels had dug in. A consulting stonemason suggested that due to the quality of materials or workmanship used during the original construction process, the pedestal would not have stood the test of time, even without the townsfolk's intervention.[22]

The Parks Department announced that the sign-up sheet would be closed imminently, then announced that time slots would be doubled and tripled up in that closing period in response to public outcry. Teenagers flocked to the spot for selfies

---

22 Their official reports used the terms "shoddy" and "rushed."

and short, stilted videos. They allowed their friends to climb up alongside them, until this was deemed to be a violation of policy. Local politicians used their influence to secure spots on the waning schedule, so that they could pose and gesture for campaign photos. A Black descendant of the general himself had a time slot donated to her[23] and reported that standing on her ancestor's former perch felt *stupid*.

The pedestal's very last official occupant was a newborn named Jerry, whose parents had signed him up prenatally and then induced labor so that he could begin his life momentously. The newspapers ate this up, though onlookers reported discomfort with seeing an infant hoisted onto a crumbling platform and also offered that his parents should have given him a few days to shape up, maybe, seeing as how he still looked unappealingly withered and squashed. When Jerry awoke atop the pedestal and began to cry, his new mother realized that she needed to feed him and also that she had not brought any accessories—a scarf or blanket or even a loose shirt—to facilitate this. She was a conservative young woman, and both she and onlookers grew flustered about the best way to appease her baby, perched and squalling in a position of such great height and consequence.[24]

At last, the pedestal was officially closed, first cordoned off

---

[23] By the same resident—a well-meaning but overzealous white woman—who had initially suggested that minority residents be given extra time on the pedestal.

[24] Young Jerry, hungry and enraged, was said to bear a passing resemblance to the general's statued visage.

with caution tape as if the spot were suddenly hazardous, and then simply left bare as public attention shifted away. The online fundraiser fell short of its goal and refunded the money back to donors. The public vote on a replacement statue closed out with "Other" as the winner.[25] In the end, it was visited regularly only by its caretaker, who had seen to the general and Whicket for three decades, along with the other statues and monuments throughout Aberdeen, one of which was of a tugboat wheel and another of which memorialized a Nazi scientist who had defected to the U.S. during the Cold War.[26]

The caretaker had shifted his focus to the pedestal almost entirely during its time in the public eye. It was he who had wiped away the bird shit and sandwich condiments and paint splatters that befell the stone. He who had scrubbed at the remaining graffiti long after it was sensible to do so, in the hopes that some chemical compound in recent rainfall might prove him wrong. After the initial protests, when the general and Whicket were still standing, the caretaker had wiped them clean of egg splatter, had undraped the toilet paper strung around them like Spanish moss. It was the caretaker who collected the discarded trash atop and beneath the pedestal, as well as throughout the surrounding park where onlookers had gathered to observe it. It was his job to see to the pedestal, and he'd done so for long enough that it took more energy to question it than it did to carry the task out.

---

25 The majority of write-ins had not specified who the "Other" should be.
26 The local YMCA's aquatics center is also named in the Nazi's honor.

It's the caretaker who can still be seen, on occasion, sitting atop the pedestal in the middle of the park, mopping at his brow with a worn handkerchief, his dark[27] skin dewy with sweat and grime and gleaming against the light that graces that weathered stone. It's as good a place as any to catch a sunset, or at the very least, the smallest sense of peace.

---

[27] Black.

SALT

FROM FAR OFF, IT LOOKS like water. Like a lake in defiance of the desert around it: impossible. Through the cracked windows of a village combi, a woman—in this case, our Alleen—seeing a salt pan for the first time, might think, *Yes*. Might think, *Here*. She might see that flat scab seared into rippled land and believe it holds something for her children. After the road and the life leading to it—all of it unspectacular and harsh—she might see it stretch into the distance and think, *This is a place of beginnings*, though she'd be at least half wrong. She'd not be the first to try to make a life here, nor the last.

The trip from town had only offered dust, the sand everywhere and always: along the gravel road they traveled on, pocked with scraggy, desperate scrub; rock and reddened grit kicked up by the village transport's wheels, surging through its worn undercarriage; still more drifting through the splintered windows, piling up in the seams. Alleen and the other passengers cocooned themselves as best they could. They wrapped their hair with fabric, wore sleeves—their skin already dulled where it lay exposed. Mothers tucked children into the sweltering tents of their skirts to keep them fresh and safe and clean.

But still, the dust found them.

The grit lined the slick skin of their nostrils and throats, climbed inside. Despite sunglasses and scarves, it pooled in the gummy pockets of their eyes. The wisest passengers found rest, despite the onslaught, and slept along with the blood in their cramped limbs. The wakeful sipped beer and soft drinks to coax the sand down, believing that sugar and carbonation worked best at tamping the itch in their throats. The dust was constant and pressing and rushing through the heat, and then—with that glimpse of a bright, flat white spooling into view—suddenly finite. Such blistered eyes might see the pan as hope.

The pan's first settlers had thought much the same. A roaming people, that wide breadth of salt—made pearly and pure by the light bouncing off it—lured them like insects to flame, stilled their tired feet. They set down their burdens and learned the edges of the anomaly, where its white met the red desert sands. The pan, then, played host to wilder beasts than them as well. Before the bushmen and their children hunted it bare, flitting springbok and proud, thick eland roamed freely, sapping minerals from the earth with dewy tongues. Predators crouched in the scrub and prowled the fringes for smaller, weaker things, venturing to center only when the need came, until men claimed their skins, too.

Before this, the pan held water—was a great, briny body teeming with life in balance with the sun above. Creatures slithered and slipped through its depths until the whims of nature shifted—who can say why?—and heat ravaged that basin too quickly for rain to compensate. Now, salt is the only standing remainder—both solid and delicate. Just below it, tightly packed layers of clay hold the bones of unfathomable life. A thin barrier of salt to bind it, preserve it. Only that.

At the slightest provocation—a downpour, which is rare but not impossible in a desert, a land prone to extremes—the pan could remake itself again. No longer stable ground, but a starved and sucking pit.

When Alleen comes to it, the land appears empty and desolate. But the pan remembers itself, remembers all it's held before her. It has a history. Of beginnings, yes. But of endings, too.

The pan, up close, was gray. Alleen told the driver to bring her straight to it, to take only their bags to the bakery where they were meant to stay. The driver, who was ready for his own bed, his wife, or else the beer bottle sweating in the village shop's half fridge, had done so without comment. And now, up close, Alleen was disappointed.

Cattle at the perimeter, lowing and licking at the salty edges, had sullied the ground beneath them. The pale earth was cracked and dirty, smudged with their tracks and dung. A lone donkey limped away from Alleen and the children, its tracks made strange by the length of rope tied around its front hooves. It screeched its strange, low song until the sound and the sight of it slipped back into the bush.

The children were giddy and writhing with energy after the confines of the trip, and so Alleen let them wander. Simeon coaxed his sister toward a herd of cattle. "Not scared?" he taunted with his hands out, beckoning. He walked with his back to the cows, but Alleen could see that his muscles were tensed and ready. Hers were city children, unfamiliar with the bounds of threat or friend in a place like this.

Lani shook her head and ran after her brother. They charged the herd together. The nearest heifer stood her ground, only turning a large head to watch the oncoming children, who dug their heels in before they reached her. They squealed and ran away, repeated the game until Alleen called them back.

She looked into the distance and took up their hands. Together, they set out, walked farther into the pan until the land was only white. Until the ground crunched thickly beneath their feet and broke into pieces. Alleen turned a slow circle at the pan's center as the children lifted the brittle panes of it to their mouths to taste.

Before nightfall, they arrived at the bakery. Alleen's cousin, confused by the bags that had arrived at her doorstep alone, had carried them inside by herself. The welcome dinner she'd prepared for them had long gone cold—the fat of the meat now solid and pale. Alleen apologized but did not explain in detail. The trip there had been long, she said. They were tired. She and the children took their meal in the cousin's spare bedroom, and the children fell asleep immediately afterward, with grease still on their fingertips.

Kneading dough was a task best performed with one's attention fixed somewhere in the distance, and over the next few weeks, Alleen shaped a plan for her family. *Join us!* the cousin called out on breaks, when the women unrolled fatcakes and lounged on upturned crates. This, before she knew that Alleen intended to turn away her kindness, the hospitality of a room and a roof over their heads, given simply because Alleen had asked for it. She and Alleen had not been close as children, but family was family; blood was blood. The bakery had grown busier with orders than she and the others could keep up with, and Alleen was in need of a fresh start. How was the cousin to predict that a barren stretch of land, which belonged to no one and shouldn't, could look to Alleen like something more?

When the cousin finally learned what was to come, she was sullen, insulted. She dropped bread pans on the table rather than hand them to Alleen, turned her back to her at break time and let the other women follow suit. She did not take the job away and for this, at least, Alleen was grateful. She could withstand the rest.

Alleen learned the village was split by the pan at its center, with tribes on either side. Each insisted their land was superior—that green lurked beneath the scrub on their side of the pan, that their rocks were smaller and more manageable. Each swore their language better suited the tongue, claimed their children would give *their* traditions lasting power. But both called the pan *Omongwa*.

It called to Alleen, like an incantation: Omongwa. She repeated it while she tried to convince a lone few men to build a home there for her. A simple tin shack, she said. Omongwa, pointing behind her. Out there, amid the salt.

They might have wondered what kind of woman would choose such a life. Out there, alone. Maybe a strange kind of woman—the kind they should keep far away from their own homes. Out there, on the pan, where she couldn't do them any harm. After enough bills spilled from Alleen's pockets and enough petitions from her lips, the men agreed to try.

Abandoned dwellings littered the pan's perimeter, and the men loaded the remnants into trucks and donkey carts, hauled them toward the pan's center. There would be no solid foundation, they warned her; no concrete slab, since they would not, could not pour one there. No matter, Alleen told them. The salt had drawn her there, and she would be closer to it this way. The men gouged the swatch of salt she'd designated and stood metal sheeting up in the cracks.

They built her legend, too. The men gossiped freely in their mother tongues as they worked, even after Alleen and the children returned with their few belongings at day's end. When their looks turned lustful, Alleen found the height and swell of a commanding posture. A woman alone—even a maybe-crazed one—could never be too careful.

The men pieced together the walls of the house in one day, an outhouse behind it the next. They left the remaining tin piled up on the ground, promising to finish the roof the following day. Alleen told them to bring paint with them when they returned. White, she said, like the pan. She didn't call it hers.

When they'd left, Alleen unloaded what she and the children had carried there—clothing, a cast-iron pot, canned meat, tins of tea and spices. She sent Simeon to gather wood before dark, and she and Lani designated rooms with the belongings they lined against the shelter's walls: their bedroom here, and the place for everything else, just here. When night fell, she and the children slept exposed to the elements, wary not of the creatures that might call the pan home, but of the men who did not.

We might say here what she is running from. To come to a mineral blight in the desert and claim it could hint, to some, of desperation. To take her children from all they knew must mean the alternative was something terrible.

But it is not so.

In the life before the one she is choosing now, Alleen was mother and lover—or at the very least, bed-warmer. She was a daughter, a niece and cousin. She woke to the children's father on the mattress beside her or elsewhere, most likely in the bed of the woman who had married him and cherished him and had built a home and brood of children to orbit around him. Alleen rose and made her children breakfast and sent them to school. She did the washing, roused an aunt from a spirit-soaked stupor and bid her to wash the liquor's stench from the back of her neck. She cleaned and swept their compound and threw scraps to the gaggle of pups (or simply thin and stunted dogs; who could say how long they'd been this way?) that cowered and snapped by the firepit. The children returned or their father returned, or some other relative appeared to ask something more of Alleen until the moment she lay down, only for the day to repeat itself.

There were women just like Alleen all over town, women

who went from girls to mothers and wives, who kept their hair wrapped and bodies round until they became the old women of their households, and therefore children again, prone to mischief. Alleen could see her future in each of theirs.

One evening, the children's father called to say he could not visit them any longer, that his wife was angry at the money slipping from his pockets to pay for Simeon's and Lani's school shoes—their feet would only keep growing, the wife said, keep demanding more and more from him until her children went bare and beggared. Was that what he wanted? Their babies with calloused feet?

A call like this one came every few months. Inevitably, he would tire of his wife's attentions and slink back to Alleen. This time, Alleen said to stay gone. She and the children would move to the village, she said, stay with a cousin who had work for her. They would start anew. And anyway, was he sure her children were his? They called him Sir, not Father, Alleen reminded him, and their faces carried no trace of his—hadn't he noticed? Better to end the lie now.

She hung up the call before he could answer and bolted the doors in case he came to see if it were true. She did not cry or waver in her bed alone that night. In the morning, she packed up her belongings and children and booked a car, then left without asking anyone if she should.

In the pan, Alleen does not find a lonely place, or at least not only lonely. From its center, she can see visitor or stranger coming well before they arrive, can raise her children as she pleases, and set the rhythm of her days. Here, Alleen's future is her own. For a woman whose name means alone in the first place—bestowed by a mother bleeding out of the world Alleen was entering—the pan's lonely is a fitting home.

By the time the builders returned a week later, Alleen had grown accustomed to the rhythm of days on the pan—to the sun's path from one side to the other, then around and back again. They added the roof, fit and nailed the simple structure together. One man lingered after he'd been paid, did not drive away with the others but took a seat by the fireside instead. He seemed to Alleen to be the crew's leader, but perhaps he was only the tallest among them, the one most likely to grow louder whenever Alleen drew near.

Simeon and Lani had long scampered away. Alleen poured a drink for the man from the jerry can she and the children had labored to carry there—a short glass, lest he consider it reason to stay longer. The well at the pan's edge was an hour's walk there and back. Its water stung with brine: potable, but uninviting—a taste Alleen was struggling to grow accustomed to, but that served her now.

The man took the cup and drained it, made a face and sucked his teeth. He seemed burdened with talk and let it flow out of him without Alleen's bidding, with little participation from her at all. He told her of the misfortunes he'd suffered, how his schooling was unfinished and his hands cracked and rough from the life he led. He pulled a flask from his pocket and offered it to her, but Alleen shook her head. She kept her eyes on him as he spoke, but

pivoted the softer parts of herself away. What she'd built here—
not with her hands, but in spirit, with her own, thick will—had
no place for him. Men, she'd found, were prone to leaving unless
ordered to, in which case they hunkered down. Alleen told this
man she'd pray for him, that she would remember to bless him in
her prayers alongside her family.

"I hope it will be enough, sister," he said. He glanced then at
the door of her home—after all, just a thin sheet of metal, closed
with wire he'd bent himself. Perhaps he considered the ease of
taking her, the luster of her skin beneath his own ashen limbs.
But what kind of woman was she to build a home on the pan? He
might have contemplated the contagion of lunacy, the hot meal
waiting for him at his own fireside. "I should be going," he said,
standing to leave.

Alleen unknotted.

The man climbed into his truck, turned the engine over a few
times. Once it started, he leaned out of his open window. "Something to remember me by," he said, flicking something in Alleen's
direction that landed at her feet. She remained standing, refused
to bend in his presence. Alleen held his eye until he pulled away.

Alleen let the moment settle across her skin. She stooped
to retrieve what he'd tossed—a matchbook, still mostly full. She
tucked it into her skirt pocket, then gathered up the brush and
paint the builders had left behind. She covered the mismatched
tin, made it uniform. The fading light bounced off the pan and
her fresh, new home, sunset's colors tinting both. She called out
when she was finished and her voice carried to where the children
played and brought them back to her.

A week later, the same man returned bearing gifts. He un-loaded blankets and more water, cans of food, wrapped biltong. The man talked rapidly of an uncle without children who'd died and willed him cattle and land. Though he spoke of misfortune, it was clear the man was glad. He thanked Alleen for the good she had brought him.

Alleen told the children to carry the gifts inside. She was puzzled by what the man thought she had done for him but wise enough to accept the spoils. She remained quiet, nodded when he looked to her for response, waved his truck away when he left. By the time he'd finished his first beer at the village shebeen, Alleen was a woman living on a salt flat, possibly capable of magic.

When word traveled that Alleen was anything more than crazy, the villagers were slow to believe it. The two sides were united in their hesitation. Who among them still believed in witchcraft? *Ha!* They were not their grandmothers, not children. Not some poor, halved souls drinking themselves dry each evening and claiming their misfortune stemmed from crossing the wrong kind of person. The only will enacted was the will of God. Weren't they good and faithful Christians?

Mothers warned their children to stay away from Alleen's, but the pan siblings grew more popular by forbiddance. Their lure extended to both sides of the village, unchecked by tribal division. The boy taught theirs to make slingshots, to shoot a bird right from the sky. The girl was small and sweet, and even the mothers caught themselves wiping the dust from her face before remembering to whom she belonged. If the mothers weren't watching closely, the pan children drew theirs to it, to play at the perimeter. Once they'd returned home to meet their mothers' discipline, the village children swore they had not ventured toward the woman at the center. The pan siblings had warned them away, they said. The salt pan woman would not allow children besides her own to come close.

The women imagined they could see the house from their windows. Or on their way to the shop—to the school. Her house a ridge in the broad, flat white. The dark spot of the firepit. The sharpest eyed among them claimed they could see Alleen herself, milling around her small compound.

They did not speak to her when she was in town, at the bakery or leaving it. The shopkeeper avoided her eye when Alleen bought matches or cooking oil or pap. When the shopkeeper put out her hand for payment, it appeared there, always without Alleen touching her skin—as if the pan woman, too, was wary. The longest look any of them dared to get, in the beginning, was of Alleen's back turned to them, trudging toward the center of the pan. Even then, there was the slightest hitch in her step, which made it seem like she might pivot around at any moment and catch them staring.

They wondered if she could feel them watching. From their more adventurous youth, they remembered how the village appeared from the pan's depth—how one could discern the whole of the world around them, made miniature and insignificant. Perhaps the pan woman was watching them, too.

Some ventured to the center out of curiosity. Out of bravery, or what they claimed was kindness. They returned and reported that the woman there was quiet, a bit stern. They said she asked nothing and expected them to fill the silence. They laughed and shook their heads at the power it was rumored she held. They hadn't seen it, they said. Not every strange woman has something worthwhile to offer.

But their figures were slimmer than when they'd set out. Whatever they'd tucked into their pockets or the bags they'd carried with them was gone when they returned, had been left behind at the middle.

Those first few months are hot and bare but blissful for Alleen, not because they're without challenge but because the challenges are new. The flow of visitors grows steadily. Twice a week, Alleen pauses in household chores to receive someone—asking for fortune, for relief, for respite from sin. Occasionally, a visitor drives in from town. She promises nothing but her attention, and for many, that seems enough.

Alleen stores and cooks the food they bring her, fills her simple home with gifts from people who believe their talking—their need—demands something physical in return. Alleen does not correct them. Why turn away a blessing that asked so little of her? Why tell the visitors that she's only ever shaped dough and her children, never a fate besides her own?

A man with a rotting, painful tooth brought Alleen a radio, and from then on, a gospel keening filled the background of her meetings. A devout young woman who asked to see God brought

Alleen money taken from her father's wallet. Alleen counseled patience as the highest virtue and used the funds to pay her children's school fees.

There is one unwelcome visitor to the pan—a black cat who lurks at the edge of Alleen's vision or else lounges in full view. It grooms its dark fur in the shade her house casts, captures prey between its palms. Scorpions, spiders. Once, a dark rope of snake. Alleen, upon seeing the cat, throws whatever object is at hand, sends the cat scampering across the salt. She knows the children feed the animal scraps when she is not looking, perhaps aim softer words in its direction. But one pest breeds another. The cat is an omen of bad luck, and she will not let it spoil her pan.

In time, her job at the bakery grows as unnecessary as it is hostile. One sweltering afternoon when school has let out for its midday break, Lani comes to her mother at work. There are fresh, hot loaves cooling or trying to, and Lani darts at the crust of one. She pulls away a chunk to reveal the loaf's soft middle and before Alleen can scold the child, the cousin swats Lani, knocks the bread from her hand. Lani does not cry out but looks at her prize on the ground, now sandy and ruined, good for no one. The baker's own children are given a loaf to split each day, to sop the grease from their lunches or to dip into their milk. Even now, the children of the other workers stand at the door, frozen on the path to take away the loaves that are daily theirs.

Alleen takes a breath. It would be beneath her to make a scene, she reasons. The cousin avoids her eye. There are several months' worth of unspoken words between the women, the pressure high and mounting. Alleen takes up three bagged loaves and her daughter's hand, and that is the end of it. She will not return to the bakery. The cousin will find a way to send her last paycheck.

Alleen decides on her final walk back to the pan—final because she does not intend to leave it again, will remain in her place at its center—that she is better for this sharp, severing moment. She and the children will build what they need to survive and the rest will find them—carried in the arms of people asking for small miracles and leaving with little more than hope. Alleen begins granting counsel to more visitors wishing for changes in luck, health, family. She agrees to pray for everything but rain.

Then, winter.

The nights are longer, somehow crueler than when they were too hot to sleep through. The wind and cold sneak through the seams of their home, threaten to turn their fingers and toes brittle. Alleen huddles the children against her. She and Simeon sleep wrapped around Lani, and though the cocoon of her family makes her sweat, Lani keeps still for the warmth she must give them, too.

In the mornings, Alleen wakes first and rises to rub the gray from the children's feet. She removes their socks and cups her palms around their soles, breathes whatever heat is inside of her out onto their skin. The children wake as the feeling comes back to the ends of them, and when their eyes crack open to find her crouched at the end of the bed, Alleen scurries her fingertips against their newly tingling arches. Both child and parent pretend the affair of the night before was a means to this game. On some mornings, the laughter escapes them in puffs.

The cat draws closer in the cold. Just beyond the house's threshold, Alleen finds dark brown spots of blood seeped into salt. Sometimes parts—tails or beaks or husks—of prey she cannot identify and doesn't care to. She shudders, then sweeps the remains toward the trash pile before the children can see.

The cat's coat stands out against the white around it, and Alleen can often spot it in the distance, trotting toward the edge or back. It seems the animal, too, can see her from afar, and the two spend whole afternoons aware of the other, both prowling the circumference of what they've claimed as theirs. One night, she awakens to its bright eyes gleaming inside the house. She shouts and reaches for a flashlight, but in the glow of the beam and the children's confusion, there's nothing to be found. Only a dream, she tells herself. She sleeps again, but fitfully.

Alleen's wishers bring blankets with them. They bring firewood and thin socks that she layers over the family's cracked heels before nightfall. The heat of midday makes the children forget what's coming, and when they return one evening with socks and shoes damp, Alleen slaps them harder than she intends.

"What's this, eh? You want to freeze?"

The two stand gripping their cheeks. Tears well in Lani's eyes, but she works to keep them from spilling—a new impulse for a child whose tears were once a sudden storm, quick to fall in unpredictable bouts. Alleen regrets slapping them before her palm is done stinging. But the two of them must learn.

Simeon takes his hand down from his face, kneels to untie his laces. There is something of his father in the set of his jaw, despite Alleen's claim to see none of him there.

"It was only the well, Ma," he says. "We were playing."

He works the shoes off his feet, then the socks, and walks barefoot to the fireside to hang them. Lani follows, walking to her brother before bending down to remove her shoes so Alleen does not see her cry.

A different sort of bravery brews at the pan's rim. The shopkeeper grows tired of watching her father suffer. He is old, though the woman could not say his age, exactly. The skin of his face and hands is so wrinkled it's almost smooth, like a paper sack crumpled and flattened again and again. His limbs have bent and drawn close to his body, and his mouth puckers tight against gums. He has not spoken since a bad fall weeks before, but he pours a steady moaning into the frosty air of his room each night, keeping the rest of the family awake.

The village hospital has counseled the shopkeeper to be patient. Death comes slowly to some. The shopkeeper slips tablets of Panadol into her father's lips each night. She tucks hot water bottles into his blankets and swaddles him as she did her babies. But the night howl continues, even strengthens. It draws dogs to their door. Each morning, she finds that her father still breathes and the crescents under her children's eyes—her own—have etched deeper.

After too many mornings like this, the shopkeeper visits Alleen. She goes on foot to give herself time to turn back. She fears witchcraft the way many of the villagers do—as if it is a flu they might catch despite their efforts. But her feet carry her to the compound and back by midday. The shopkeeper is quiet when she returns, and friends and patrons cluck their tongues. They say that she's been witched.

But it's guilt, not ill luck, that bears down on the shopkeeper—guilt for asking the woman to kill her own father. "Please," she begged of Alleen. "We must have peace."

For three nights, the old man's vigil continues. When it stops, no one in the household is the wiser. They sleep heavily, burrow deep in the rest they're owed. The silence will wake them when they're ready.

The shopkeeper rises first, finds her father cold. Without alerting the others, she sets out toward her shop. There, she empties items from the shelves—toothpaste and lentils and chips and sweets. But the collection looks paltry. It doesn't seem like enough.

Alleen and the children spot the truck coming up the worn path to the house. The shopkeeper climbs out with a man she says is her brother. He mumbles obscenities, words for Alleen she does not want the children to hear. She sends Simeon and Lani away.

From the way the woman avoids her eyes, Alleen guesses what has happened. A wished-for thing can still be heavy. The pair walk to the truck bed and pull back a tarp, heave and lift some great bulk from it. They carry it around to a corner of the compound that Alleen points to, not too far from the house.

The shopkeeper looks at Alleen, full in the face for the first time, and nods. Her brother peers around the compound, taking stock of what he sees there. The left corner of his mouth hangs low and crooked, and Alleen is unsurprised to see him spit. The shopkeeper prods his arm and they climb into the truck and pull away.

When they've gone, the children return. They must have remained close by, watching.

"What is it, Ma?" they ask, circling the machine.

"A chance," Alleen says. "Life."

The generator is so dead and quiet that both children wonder what she means.

When word spreads that Alleen can bring death, the number of visitors spikes. A jealous lover pays her a heater; a schoolteacher in long, thick extension cords. In a week, an inheritance dispute brings her enough gasoline to run the generator through winter, and she and the children fall asleep to its metal hum each night.

Alleen tracks the children's growth by sight. Simeon is eleven and reedy, squirms beneath her gaze. The knot in his throat that will make his voice a man's has only just begun to grow. He is secretive when he undresses for bed and bathing, hides his body as a growing boy should from his mother. But Lani is still young enough to crave touch. She comes running each time her mother calls, twirls in Alleen's hands. Once, Alleen spots a long scratch across Lani's wrist and her daughter covers it, runs away when Alleen asks what made it.

Alleen means to protect her children from what would bring them harm. She searches for dark and hidden places where the cat might take refuge, but finds nothing. She strings pots and pans up on the laundry line, so the racket will scare it away. When she spots the cat standing on its back paws under the line the next day, swatting at the pots with its claws, Alleen runs out with her kitchen knife. The cat hears her coming above the sound of clanging iron and takes off, faster than she can follow. In this way, she and the cat pass the time on the pan, in what one considers battle and the other makes play.

On a still, blue day, a girl arrives to ask for rain. She is tall, with cheekbones that catch the light and throw it back. There is an air about her Alleen finds disrespectful, though in truth, she and the girl are more alike than not. The girl carries newspapers and money with her, holds them both out in offering, but Alleen crosses her arms. Only the newspaper will be useful in drawing out the fire for their dinners, though plastic bags would do the job more quickly. Alleen has enough money buried in the house's secret places and too much of it makes them vulnerable, might draw the wrong kind of visitor.

"Please, Ma," says the girl. "I've heard about your rules, but you must change them. You must make this one exception."

Alleen does not even waste her tongue to speak.

The young woman is undeterred. She spreads out a newspaper on the table between them. The headline reads simply, "Drought." Such a useless proclamation in a land like theirs, Alleen thinks.

Only a week before, a cow had dropped dead on the pan from heat. Alleen scolded Simeon for venturing close to see it, then sent him back with a knife and a bucket, lest the meat lying there go to waste. He returned with little. He said the cow's ribs pressed against the curves of its hide, that its hips were pointed beneath the skin—had almost pierced through in its fall to the earth. Others had come, too, to slice meat from the bone, and Simeon had run back home, carting his spoils—whatever castoffs the others had left. He knew his mother would want the tongue, but he could not bear to cut it from a still-warm mouth.

"What kind of ears do you have, girl?" Alleen asks now, breaking her silence. "The others must have warned you about my rules."

There are stories of the pan gone soft with rain. Rumors that, once, it swallowed a truck whole—pulled the weight straight down in seconds. This drought has stretched long, rendered the ground dry and hard and the villagers' memory of anything else scant. But Alleen—as well as the life she's built there—requires the pan firm. She crumples the newspaper and stands to shoo the girl away.

"The rains will come," the girl warns as she goes. "They're coming even now—you must feel it."

Both women pause, perhaps waiting for the telltale wind against their skin.

"I am only asking you to bring them sooner."

Alleen makes a noise in her throat and turns away. She marches inside and shuts the door behind her. She watches through the window as the girl sets off across the pan on foot, growing smaller in the distance.

Alleen fears what the girl has asked for, what the girl will tell the others. She does not go so far as to admit she fears the girl herself. If others begin to ask for the same and Alleen refuses, will they grow angry with her? Stop visiting? She looks across the expanse of salt, which is clear but for the day's heat wriggling off its surface. She listens for a rumble of thunder, hears only the distant jingle of bells around the necks of cattle.

By dinnertime, Alleen has already begun to ration supplies. She considers how much water the children will need rather than want, which foods will fill them quickest. The porridge tonight will be thick, but manageable. Alleen sets the newspaper on the wood beneath the pot, watches the headline catch and blacken in the crackling flame.

For the world at the perimeter, the heat has taken its toll. Any growth is stalled to a halt. The brackish pond at the edge of the pan is long dry, the bed of it parched and cracked apart like lips. The people carry buckets of water to their livestock and stand looking at the sky for a hint of change.

After he reads in print what the ribs of his sheep have already told him, a headman calls a meeting. He gathers men from both sides of the pan at the hospital, which is neutral ground.

"When was the last good rain?" the headman asks those who have gathered. Hadn't the pond at the pan's rim been dwindling since the woman's arrival?

Something must be done.

The villagers are worn thin. Theirs has been a dry land for as long as they can remember, but not a dying one. They agree with the headman. Something must be done, and why not this: they will send the headman's daughter to demand that the woman at the pan's center bring the rain she is keeping from them. They send the sharp-cheeked girl, the very girl Alleen will spurn.

When Alleen will not ask for rain, they reason she brings its opposite. In those early days, they'd seen her around the village, working bread and limping home. Just a woman then. The villagers are not prepared for violence, but they'll play to the woman's magic—work a conjuring of their own. They imagine that what-ever magic she possesses comes from the land beneath her, that she has drawn it into herself from their pan. But no one can keep watch always. Now, at the helm of something larger than herself, perhaps the woman's grip is slacker than she knows. It may unfurl from her grasp while she's sleeping, might slip away in wisps. The pan was theirs to begin with, wasn't it? Might its will be made theirs too?

They are wrong, of course, to think the land is anything to be harnessed or bent to a desire besides its own. For the pan, the heat is as it's always been: unending until it's not.

Lani searches the salt flat for treasures. Fewer visitors come to the house now—maybe one every other week—and as the drought takes up more and more of their worry, the villagers have begun leaving talismans against it. Money caught under cups of water—always paper bills, always glass. Some with water still puddled within and others dry and empty, a mineral rim at their bottoms. Lani is excited by the game of it, by messages she cannot understand. She leaves the charms where they stand. One day she leads her mother by hand to a charm not far from their compound, but Alleen is not at all glad to see it. She does not bend to retrieve it, but spits onto the salt beside it, which quickly draws the moisture in.

Alleen is angry with the boldness of the rain wishers and their shrinking proximity to her, to the center of the pan. What might a greedy earth do with the weight of a home? With their lives there? The rain would undo them, both in fact and legend.

Alleen has refused to call for rain, and so its arrival would prove her power a lie.

The rain wishers come most often by night—on foot, too afraid to drive over the ground they pray will soften. Alleen is short with those who visit by day, her nerves thin. Have they asked for rain, too, left something to litter the pan?

"Tell the others to keep their distance," she warns. "Tell them to come and face me."

Alleen grows richer each day with the talismans left across her pan, but she cannot leave to trade money for food—will not walk through a village turned against her. She is determined that for the pan to hold, she must hold its center.

Still, the air thickens. Wind kicks up grains of salt and sand, sends them skittering across the sides of the house. On some afternoons, the grit pelts Alleen and drives her inside where she listens to it rush against the tin. She wonders where the children are, if they've found cover. She begins to draw Simeon and Lani closer, does not let them play with other children. The colors wrapped around the sun at day's end are darker, more bruised and drab.

How long can a whole sky hold?

She and the children drag the mattress outside to catch a cooling breeze while they sleep. One night, Alleen wakes to a high, building screech that sends her blood humming. She sits up, tries to pick where the shrieking might be coming from, but it's all around her. It whips across the nape of her neck, flits through the hairs on her arms. The full moon casts her pan bright but wrong in the nightmare sound. Alleen can feel the rawness of the throat it comes from, and she swallows. There is a high pitch and then a last low growl, and then nothing. Quiet.

In the silence, Alleen thinks she might have imagined the sound. Only a dream, she thinks. She'll need rest for the day ahead. She picks out the bundles of her still-sleeping children curled beside her in the moonglow and lies back, breathes to slow the trill of her heartbeat. She finds sleep again.

In the morning, a woman is waiting, just beside the bed.

"Sorry, Ma," she says when Alleen wakes and sees her. "I don't mean to frighten you."

Alleen sucks air to begin shouting about privacy and space, but stops herself. Their food stores are low, and she cannot afford to turn anyone away. Instead, she stands up, prods the children awake. They don't startle at the sight of the woman waiting—hardly ever do at the appearance of visitors. Perhaps for the children, the pan is less a lonely place. They stretch and wipe night from the corners of their eyes, trudge toward the firepit to begin breakfast.

Alleen beckons for the woman to step inside, offers her a chair. The woman is swollen with child. Her belly hangs low, like it might slide away from the thin body supporting it. The seat of the chair seems to stall this threat momentarily.

The woman asks, unsurprisingly, for a safe birth. She cites the list of bad omens received already, the shell of an infant she lost before. Alleen places a hand on the hard globe of the woman's stomach and promises to think of her in the coming weeks. She soothes her as best she can and by the time they have talked through the past and into the baby's future again, the day has grown dark and gloomy. Alleen sees her out, distracted. She forgets to ask for payment, and the woman does not remind her. The wind, for the moment, is still, and Alleen watches the woman dwindle in the distance as she limps away.

And then the disturbance of the night comes back to Alleen. The screech rips through memory and Alleen turns back toward the house, trying to sort her recollection of the night before into dream and reality. In her path are droplets of blood—small and scattered, like rust. They wind away from her and Alleen squints to see them in the day's grim light. She follows their trail to the back of the house, toward the rubbish pit.

Someone has traded blood for rain. They have reasoned, perhaps, that water is too thin a talisman and offered, instead, what only the living can give. The cat: dead and gone for hours now, the red of it still leaching into the salt. Its fur—black as luck—is matted, its face turned away from her.

The first few drops are warm. The rain lands on Alleen and the salt, on the knife-torn creature. Somewhere, raindrops bead upon her children and swaybacked animals. Past the pan's edge, they grace upturned palms and faces, heedless of side or tribe. The air presses against Alleen like breath and already, she senses a new give to the ground beneath her feet—a softening away from what she feels it promised her. And the fall could be light, brief. But there is a history here of change. A record of impermanence. Alleen calls out for her children, and her voice slips into thunder—into the distance and the landscape around her, which prepares to take its due.

GO WAY BACK

YOU'VE ARRIVED, AND HERE YOU are: on a couch in Laurel, Mississippi, in the living room of Jim and Sheila Murray—strangers to you besides the fact that they've raised the boy you're here with, the young man who's driven you across the state to meet his parents, though you've only been dating a short while, and though *dating* was a loose term at first for the thing you were doing until he called you his girlfriend at a party in someone's off-campus apartment and you didn't correct him. A love story, of sorts, and it's brought you here and now.

Carter isn't sitting beside you. It could be unintentional, but it's hard to say for sure. There's a history between you now. He's settled into a recliner that has its own cupholder, his father in an identical chair on the other side. You and Carter's mother are wedged between them on a love seat, all of you turned to face the television in the room, which is off. You sense that this is rarely the case, that the TV was, perhaps, cut off just before you arrived and still idles—that the men and the seating are primed for its resurrection. It gives you the feeling that you've interrupted something. There could very well be a game on. It seems like there almost always is. Carter can watch anything with such enthusiasm that you'd think he knew each of the players personally.

You should say that his parents seem nice. Carter honked as the two of you pulled up, and they came out to meet you in the driveway. His mother hugged him and then you, just beside the heat-soaked truck, the exhaust fan still panting into thick air. His father lifted your bag out from the cab to carry it inside, though you'd told him not to worry about it.

"I'm stronger than I look," he'd said. He patted you on the shoulder as he passed by, said, "Relax," and you thought you'd better—sure, right, nothing here to worry about.

They'd picked at Carter's driving on the way inside, said you were taking your life into your hands with him at the wheel. You'd laughed along at their good-natured ribbing of their only son and deflected any fuss that came your way, politely—*Sure, no thank you, I'm fine*—until you found yourself here, beside his mother on the couch. The glass of sweet tea beside you sweats into its coaster.

Above you, there's a saying stickered to the wall that reads, *Live, Laugh, & Love in God*. It seems to be encouraging you to undertake these actions *inside* of God. You think of this saying—no doubt mass-produced—gracing the walls of a million houses like this one, urging dwellers to climb right into the body of Christ.

His mother asks what you're studying, if you like it, how busy your semester is. You tell her that you're technically undeclared—that your official major reads *Undecided*—but you've built up enough credits to switch over to something soon. Maybe English or psychology, philosophy. A liberal art, which is a strange name for the category—a trigger description in the South. You're taking classes to cover all of it. You've cried over your indecision in the quiet of your own dorm room, but here, you joke about it. It's only the rest of your life, you say. Easy.

"Take your time," his mother says. Then: "But not too much!"

Carter is studying engineering, the university's most commonly awarded degree. A surefire path to a stable career, it would seem. Your own father studied engineering, and the two of you no longer discuss your major: a surefire path to a fight. In your favorite class this semester, the latest assignment was to open the hood of your car and draw what you found there. The thin, wiry grad student teaching the class said that drawing from observation meant simply telling the truth. Yours had earned an A. You'd shown Carter and immediately felt embarrassed, though he'd praised you. You've tucked it away in a portfolio you won't open again for years. Hours spent on an accurately drawn car engine, for whatever that's worth.

His mother asks where you're from, if your parents still live there, if you have any siblings. She asks what your parents do.

You hesitate, thighs sticky against the sofa cushion beneath you. You worry that you'll leave a sweat mark on the pleather when you stand. It's an easy enough question—What do they do?—but you find yourself bristling.

Perhaps it's only Carter's choice of seating, or the fact that he's talking across the two of you to his father now, asking about a family friend you don't know—not even listening. Or that his mother doesn't seem bothered by this, doesn't seem distracted by the conversation volleyed over your heads.

Perhaps it's the decal on the wall and your fear that his mother will ask what church you go to—what *congregation* you're a part of—and you'll have to say that you haven't been to one in years, or else you'll lie, which is probably worse.

Perhaps it's that you don't drink sweet tea but are gulping yours now while she waits for an answer. You can feel the sugar coating your teeth.

But there's a part of you that feels protective—of your parents, your family. Of conjuring too many of their details into this room, which smells faintly of cinnamon and microwave popcorn. It's the same part of you that noticed how the hands raised in greeting as you drove into the neighborhood were pale and pink; that the kids playing in the cul-de-sac were white; that American flags waved from several front porches; that one house had a grinning lawn jockey out beside the mailbox, the statue's face painted blacker than skin. It is possible to line these details up to say nothing about a place, or everything.

And yet, despite all this, Carter's parents didn't flinch, didn't turn to each other—even for a moment—when you climbed from the car. You must have been watching for it, but there was nothing. No quick jolt of panic quickly folded into cheer. You would have seen it. Would have noticed.

Instead, they rushed to greet you. To carry your bags inside.

And this is surely because they are kind people, and welcoming, and because they're excited to meet the girl their son's been dating, however briefly. You think he must have told them something about you—must have told them a couple somethings about you, including that you're Black, or mixed. Maybe *biracial*—a word he's learned to wrap his mouth around for you. You don't want to think of it as a warning. A heads-up. Just a fact, a detail about you to go along with the others. You can't be sure he told them at all.

But with every question his mother asks, you pull back. Offer less. You feel like you are calling your family into the room for her to take a look at. To see, maybe, who's responsible for the blend, though the answer, of course, is both of them. Hardly anyone ever asks which of your parents is *white*. You want to be sitting in the room with your boyfriend's mother—impressing her, letting her get to know you. Instead, you are somewhere above the conversation, watching. Listening for cues and intentions of a thing she might not be after at all.

What do they do? You consider the combinations that might give her clues—the things your parents might do, could do:

Dentist, Barber

Preacher, Doctor

Pilot, Custodian

"One's a teacher," you say aloud, "and the other works in a lab." You keep things vague and wonder if his mother can sense the withholding. She smiles and nods, regardless. She stops asking questions. Maybe she thinks you're tired. You are tired.

If Carter's listening, he doesn't react, though he knows what your parents do—each of them, specifically. He's heard more detail with far less prompting. There is the slightest bit of blush creeping into his neck, though it could very well be the beginnings of a sunburn.

"I'm gettin hungry," he announces, like it's everyone's problem. He pats his stomach for emphasis.

"Well," says his mother, "sounds like that's my cue."

She gives your hand a little squeeze as she stands.

The men carry on talking, and she heads for the kitchen, and you wait a while longer than you would anywhere else—listen to the sink run and cabinets creak and dishes shuffle against each other—before you rise to help. As soon as you've crossed the threshold, the TV pings awake behind you, erupts with voice and noise.

Before this, half an hour from his parents' house, Carter pulls his truck into a gas station. The station's sign features a cartoon kangaroo beneath the words *Hop Away*. The sign is dingy, and the grime has crept into the kangaroo's smile, distorting it into a smirk. Its paw rests on the trigger of the gas pump tucked into its pouch. The effect is strange—both vaguely threatening and threatened. As if the kangaroo wandered into backcountry Mississippi and found a way to survive.

You'd told Carter that you didn't need to stop, that you could hold it. You'd told him that you could make it the rest of the way, but he said that would only make the problem worse. He said the bladder was a sponge that could only hold so much before it began to leak.

"Time to wring it out," he says, tossing the shifter into park at a gas station in a town you don't know the name of. Carter steps down from the cab of the truck and throws his arms wide. He arches his back, stretches his chest toward the sky. He preens in the sunlight and whoops. Actually whoops. A sliver of skin peeks from beneath his T-shirt, a line of hair marching into his jeans.

This is one of the things that drew you to him—the space that he takes up. His charm, his confidence—how close he is to comfort in any given room, which runs counter to your instincts. You imagine the two of you as a balancing act, an attraction of opposites. There is a sweet spot somewhere between you, and your relationship is a means to find it. That he is handsome and broad and strong-jawed and that he's chosen you don't hurt either. Carter is not a mystery—he is reaching for you almost always. He is driving you to meet his parents. It is not so easy to separate the want to be wanted from want itself.

Carter heads for the doors of the Roo-Mart, and you yank down the passenger-side mirror before following him. Your hair has gone wavy at the roots already, the ends bushy. Your skin, too, is oilier than usual—the unfamiliarity of straight lanks framing your face making your pores overcompensate. You tie your hair into a low bun. You lick your fingertips, try to smooth the halo of wisps around your part flat against your scalp. It's hard to tell you straightened your hair at all, even though it took hours.

Inside, there is a line for the women's restroom. There is always a line for the women's restroom. You trace lazy paths through the aisles of the shop, trying to distract your bladder. You don't pick anything up. When you were young, your mother would pull you aside at the threshold of every store.

We look with our eyes . . . , she'd say.

Not our hands, you'd finish, eyes already roaming the space.

The words play through your head like a mantra now. You were a clumsy child, prone to accidents. You'd broken things. Surely that was the reason why.

A cowboy hat bobs through the row ahead of you. A dull bushel of hair, blow-dried stiff and sticky, leans on the register. Some kids argue in Spanish over which type of candy to choose, and the lighting buzzes a thin, dull tone.

There's a rotating display in the corner that features items emblazoned with the Confederate flag: key chains, lanyards, a stuffed general in uniform with a handlebar mustache. For this, you make an exception to the rule. You take a hand from behind your back and spin the rack. There are bumper stickers and sunglasses and hats. A toddler's onesie, stamped with the stars and bars.

You wish you were the kind of girl to pull something from this rack and walk it to the register. To hold the cashier's eye as he rings you up, takes your change, all the while wondering why you'd want it. You could throw it away, then. Or wear it, turn back so they could see you in it—a thing meant against you, now yours. But you don't pick anything off the spinner. You leave the items on the rack untouched, like they would sting you if they could.

You can feel someone's attention. Eyes on you, climbing your back. But when you look up and turn around, no one's looking at you. There is only the static buzz, a murmur of conversation near the soda machine. Somewhere, a security camera plays your image across a screen. In the car, Carter will say, *No one was watching you. Nobody but me*, he'll say and smirk. He's in good spirits. He's almost home. He'll say you're just being paranoid, and maybe you are. But by the time the toilet flushes and the door to the restroom shoves open, your body has forgotten the urge to empty itself out.

Before this, Carter swats at the hand you've raised to your mouth. You've told him that your mother thinks nail-biting is a nasty habit, and now Carter has picked up the torch, though you haven't asked him to. Riding in a car is one of the activities most likely to lead your mind to wander, and your fingers too. You've torn the nail of your right thumb ragged, but it feels unfinished. You keep picking at it, hand down low beside the seat where he can't see it or slap it away.

The Red Bull buzz rushes through you from the now-empty can in the cupholder. What does taurine do for a body, to a body? You channel the energy toward the scenes passing through your window. Crooked shacks lean in close to the road, eaten through with weeds. Farther back stand the sort of houses one might call *estates*, with white picket fencing stretched over wide and rolling lawns. A few of them have horses. On some stretches, fields of tufted plants, picked over and tired, line the country road.

When you were younger, you took a field trip to a history museum. The sign beneath one display read, *Eli Whitney Invented the Cotton Gin*. You don't have a mind for dates or names, but the factoid lodged somewhere deep.

The docent held up a cotton boll for your class's inspection, showed you the raw material that fed the machine. He pointed to the leaves at the base of the plant, warned about the sharp spines standing guard within the fluff. You all passed around a neutered version—a cloud you could press to feel the seeds inside. The man took the boll and dropped it into the mouth of the machine, cranked a lever round and round until the seeds spat out at the bottom. He pulled the flattened fiber from the gin, held it up to show how it had been made useful.

"Do you know who invented the cotton gin?" you ask Carter now. Too softly. He doesn't hear you over the radio.

"Do you know who invented the cotton gin?" you ask again, louder. Carter shakes his head, then nods along with the song. He beats out a drum solo with his fingers across the steering wheel, eyes ahead. You think that when Carter sees cotton, it is maybe only a plant. Or he doesn't see it at all.

You look out the window again, try to hold one telephone pole in your vision until it's gone. You did not learn about the cotton gin at the same time you learned about slavery. History was taught in terms of heroes: slavery had Harriet Tubman, Sojourner Truth; the Industrial Revolution had Eli Whitney—a great inventor, paving the way for mass production. Whitney made cotton king, you learned, though there's no hurt tied up in the memory. No recollection of attaching that story to your skin, of linking one event to another. History was a series of disjointed happenings, devoid of cause or consequence.

There's a commercial that plays during nearly every break on TV. The actors wear cotton sundresses, cotton blouses and slacks. They ride bicycles and chase after wayward pets. The actors are white and Black and shades between. They're cheery, the graphics bright. The tagline sings, *Cotton: the fabric of our lives*. The jingle is catchy, and sometimes you sing it in the shower. It's the only advertising you can think of that isn't for a particular store—just the material itself, the crop: the fabric of our lives. A rebranding. Or the truth.

A tractor rolls by in the opposite lane, and you raise your hand and wave, though you're moving too fast for anyone riding inside to see you.

Forty miles before this, you take an exit for the back roads. The GPS estimates two hours and thirteen minutes until your final destination, but you've learned not to rely on it. The machine's harried voice cuts through the cab, sighing, urging you both to turn back. It suggests U-turns, then alternate routes that wind and scissor back toward the highway. Carter mutes the volume and you watch the screen twitch in silence, offering advice he won't heed.

"This way's nicer," he says. "You'll see."

Eventually, the machine accepts the back roads, too.

You're asking what he's told his parents about you when a squirrel darts onto the road ahead. It freezes in the middle of the lane, hesitates. Carter is flicking between radio stations, eyes down so that he doesn't see it, and you spot the plush, white belly of the thing just before it's beneath you.

You wince in preparation for the bump but there's nothing. You twist to look out the back window, expect its squashed silhouette on the road. Or the creature hopping away, crossing its tiny squirrel heart at its luck. But there's no trace of it at all.

You consider asking Carter to pull over. Telling him to. Taking the wheel and pulling the truck to the shoulder, letting the tires skip and grip across the asphalt until you're stopped. Then, climbing out and running, back to the spot where you saw the squirrel last. Bare feet slapping over the glass and gravel they're tough enough to bear.

And if there's nothing there in the road where its flattened form should be—nothing besides empty cans of Skoal and torn shopping bags caught still in the hot, stale air—you'd run back to the truck. Ignore Carter, ignore the look he'd give you and drop down to your belly to look underneath, to see if the carcass is caught in the undercarriage—its blood and fur and limbs. At least you'd know what had become of it.

And then, you might push up from the road. Shrug and say, *Overreaction*. You'd take the points of Carter's elbows into your palms and rise up on your toes to kiss him. Then climb back into the truck to buckle up, waiting until he climbs in, too, and pulls off. And he'd forgive you. He'd chalk it up to your oversensitivity, to your tender heart for animals. Every Sunday morning, you drive to the shelter to walk the stray, lonely dogs there. The barkers and jumpers and good-boys caged up and waiting. You always leave there filthy.

Instead, you stay seated, stay still. The moment—the opportunity— passes. You might have imagined the squirrel in the first place. The scene shrinks in your side-view mirror, and you let it fade.

You've fallen quiet midsentence and Carter says, "Hello? Babe?"

You reach up to unmute the GPS, and the mechanical voice

breaks through the silence of the cab between you, gasping like you've been holding her underwater. You have two hours and twenty-seven minutes left to go.

Before this, Carter pulls into the campus parking lot. You mount the step up to the passenger door and pull it open. How good can the gas mileage be for a car that practically needs a stepladder?

You ask Carter if your hair is lying flat. You've straightened it for the occasion, but in this humidity, the look is dooming fast. You ask him if you're dressed all right.

He says, "Shorts?"

The correct answer was: *You look perfect.*

You say, "Something wrong with that?" It's summertime in Mississippi, the type of weather your father calls *the air you can wear.*

He catches his mistake. "You look great," he says. "They're gonna love you just as much as I do, babe. Let's get this show on the road."

You're running late already.

He's shaved down the scruff across his cheeks and neck. You're always startled to see how young he looks when he shaves, his lips emerging baby-pink and smooth. You've told him before that it doesn't look bad—that you like him fresh and new—though in truth, you prefer the beard. You suspect that every young man resents the truth of a clean shave.

Carter plugs the address into the GPS, tucks your bag behind the seat. You have packed enough snacks for the trip ahead, but too little water.

Two nights before this, you're watching a movie together, sprawled out on your extralong twin mattress. Carter's favorite genre is Action.

You are working on a theory. You've written thesis paper after thesis paper this year, and you've learned it helps to be working on a theory almost always, to be prepared with one and ready to defend it at any given time. You theorize that the violence of modern cinema is supposed to be preventative. By showing the ways a body can be maimed and ruined, they intend to sate curiosity. By showing us the ways to wreck one another, you say to Carter, they're keeping us from trying it ourselves.

"Wreck each other, huh?" he says. He reaches under your shirt. The movie has been equal parts blood and boob, sex and death in the same loud hour. Bodies against bodies, either way.

Later, you'll revise your theory. Perhaps violence feeds the interest but doesn't satisfy it. All that blood and gore to feed the want for more of it. For now, your skin blooms against the heat from Carter's palm, and your body rises to meet it.

Two weeks before, Carter says, "Come home with me."

You don't ask him if it's too early. You don't ask how many girlfriends his parents have met before. The toothy grins of these girls still grace his old profile pictures, which doesn't bother you.

Doesn't bother you. The girlfriends favor Carter. They have dark hair like his, and freckles. You think of how seamlessly they'd fit tucked into family photos on the beach: the girls grinning in white button-ups and khaki shorts against a backdrop of sand dunes and sky.

You agree to it. You kiss Carter like he's given you something.

You've never met a boyfriend's parents. You have had very few boyfriends. In all the rom-coms, meeting the parents weighs heavy. It's a make-or-break moment. You fall asleep in his bed with your arm thrown across his chest, his heart beating against the pulse at your wrist.

The month before, his fraternity planned a decades party. You hate his fraternity. You don't understand his attachment to it. You hate the stained, dingy house. The scent of half-empty beer cans. The bare rooms with pool tables in the middle and holes punched along the walls. Disrepair seems to be the point, like they're proving all the movies right. You dread walking ahead of him there, feeling the edge of a high five passed behind your back.

Once, you sat in his frat brother's room for hours, watching the boys play a shooter video game. His frat brother introduced himself as Moose—no telling if it was a nickname or a last name. But it fit him. The boys sniped and punched and lobbed grenades at enemies. When they were ambushed, their blood spattered across the screen before they respawned.

"What war is this supposed to be?" you'd asked, and the boys— deep in concentration—hadn't answered.

A rebel flag stretched across one wall of Moose's room, emblazoned with the words *Heritage Not Hate* in camo-printed lettering. Hideous, even without the idea behind it. You'd felt their eyes on you when you'd first walked in and saw it: Moose's eyes and Carter's. A stranger who believed the argument enough to decorate with it; your boyfriend, who invited you knowing it was there, or else not knowing—maybe not even seeing it, really, until you and the flag were in the same room together.

Later, Carter will say that it must've been new. He tells you he'll say something about it to Moose, and you'll consider saying, *Too late.* Instead, you'll tell Carter not to bother on your account. There's no point in trying to save the hardheaded, and a boy named Moose is already lost.

And anyway, there in Moose's room, the decision was yours, too: how much fit to pitch, or fuss to raise. You could've turned and walked right out. Instead, you sat down in a busted office chair with yellow foam poking from the seat, with your back to the banner. You felt the pressure of held breath slip out, and the boys played on. And you'd let them.

For the decades party, Carter considers going dressed as a hippie, or as a cowboy. He settles on an '80s aerobics instructor, dons a neon windbreaker and short shorts that show the bulged muscles above his knees, the line where the bright, virgin skin of his thighs shows through.

You searched for pictures of flappers. Images of afro'd disco queens and afro'd Black Panther-ettes. You'd need to pick your hair out to pull off the look. When Carter comes to pick you up, you're not in costume. You tell him you're not feeling well. He kisses your forehead and goes alone. He tells you later that the costumes were hilarious. *Hilarious*, he said.

Nostalgia for the past is a white preoccupation. It's something you heard from a boy on the campus lawn. A boy with skin like spent coffee grounds, talking to other Black kids sprawled out on the lawn with him—who'd laughed and said, *Okay, Mr. Professor. Mr. Critical Race Theory. Calm down.* You'd kept walking, nervous they'd see you watching. You are your whitest in a Black crowd.

But you find yourself repeating the phrase. You put the emphasis in different places—now *white* now *past.* You chew the line on your walk to class, to the gym and back. You try to draw the marrow out.

Sometime before this, you nod a greeting at a stranger on the street. Once the man has passed by, Carter asks if you know him.

You consider telling him the truth of it: that you have nodded and the man has nodded because you are keeping tabs on each other, letting the other know you're there. In any given restaurant or shop, you know exactly how many Black people are there with you. You consider how it might sound to your boyfriend: conspiratorial, paranoid. Some secret, tight thread running where he can't see it.

You tell Carter no. Only that.

And so perhaps the space that lies between you, that stretches and grows, is at least half your fault.

At winter break, you pick through your parents' attic. You dig through the boxes of old clothes in search of something vintage.

Vintage is a word for something old made cool again, and the girls at school are crazy for it. Everyone is thrifting now, regardless of whether or not they could pay for the same clothes new.

You find a leather bag with flowers pressed into it like burns, a sweatshirt with the schematics of a building printed across it. There's a letter in your mother's handwriting tucked into the purse.

You wear the sweatshirt on the drive back to campus, in class, to sleep. In a month, you've stretched the neck wide enough to fit your hair without mussing it.

You leave the purse buried deep in the box, inside your parents' attic—the letter to your mother's mother refolded and tucked inside.

I know this has been hard for you and Dad, it reads, *but this is my family.*

Your granddaughter is beautiful.

Come meet her?

Before this, Carter says, "I love you."

You say it right back, because you just might. You are testing out the sound and the feeling behind it. There is a rush in your stomach when you hear it. A rush when you say it too.

You suspect that neither of you mean it quite yet, that instead you are almost-loving each other—that you can feel the space where love might fit now and each time you wake up together, each time he brings you coffee in the library, and when he lets you cut his hair. You shaved a patch too close to the scalp the first time, but you didn't mind seeing it there—the mark of you on him.

You'd like to be in love. You are approaching the feeling and maybe he is already there. It will hurt him if you don't say it, so you do: over the phone, at the high window of his truck, at parties. You both say it when you part, like it's the last time, every time.

I love you, I love you, you say it a little too often. You worry you'll wear the meaning thin.

Before this, you learn about the Stanford prison experiment.

"Impersonation leads to belief," your professor says.

You write that down. You are considering majoring in sociology. The study of human society seems to cover so much, though you're not sure what a degree in it could do. The professor plays video clips from the study while he lectures about perceived power, about groupthink and performance. You're listening too closely and you forget to write the rest down.

At midterm, you borrow Carter's notes to compare and find that he has recorded only the broadest details:

1971; 24 participants, male; mock prison, psych building base-ment.

There is nothing in Carter's cramped writing about the abuse the students called *guards* inflicted upon the students called *prisoners*—the strip searches and withheld meals, the buckets brimming with waste. No notes about the uniforms: mirrored sunglasses worn by the guards to block eye contact; dresses without underwear for the inmates, to simulate humiliation. Nothing about the prisoners called by number rather than by name, about the mental breakdowns, about how after it was over—the study cut short, terminated after only six days—researchers couldn't quite say what they'd proven.

You find that you remember the lesson well enough, without his notes or yours.

Before this, you are panting beside each other, your bodies sweating where they touch. You are still learning to catch the rhythm of thrusts, to move your hips against Carter's. When you lose the pattern, there's a stutter like the double jump of a trampoline. When you were younger, this was a good thing.

He tells you he's never dated a Black girl before, never been with anyone of color. You hate the phrase *of color*.

You admit to him that you've only ever dated white boys—boys who look like him, sound like him. Boys who look at you like he does. It's a pattern you're not proud of, though it might be something learned: this attraction to the Other, inherited.

You wonder what your bodies mean together, say together. What you might unravel with just the press of skin.

Because, of course, before this, people who looked like him owned people who looked like you—like your father and your father's mother; unlike your mother and hers. Worked, lashed, beat people who looked like you. Maimed, broke, bred people who looked like you. Hanged them; sold and raped them. And then later, kept separate, though a few—of them? of you?—stole closer.

And it is not his fault or yours. Not either of your doing. But there it lies beside you, tangled up in cotton sheets, and you are doing all you can to recover from what came before this—the history between you—but you are not sure if any of it is enough.

ACKNOWLEDGMENTS

I can't stop
my gratitude, which includes, dear reader,
you, for staying here with me,
for moving your lips just so as I speak.

—Ross Gay,
"Catalog of Unabashed Gratitude"

Ross Gay says it better, but I'll say it again: My first thanks goes to you, dear reader.

Thank you to my stellar agent, Stephanie Delman, for her unwavering belief in this collection, for the edits that made it stronger, and for her kind and expert guidance throughout the process of bringing a debut story collection into the world. Thank you to my genius editor, Rebekah Jett, for her close attention, her endless patience over even the most minute wording details, and her enthusiasm for this book and those to come. Thank you to the entire Trellis Literary team (and the extended Trellis author family), especially Khalid McCalla for his earliest reads and for keeping us all afloat. A huge thank-you to everyone on the Scribner team who helped make this book real—to those of you I've worked with directly and those behind the scenes—but especially, thanks Natalia Olbinski for *House Gone Quiet*'s beautiful face, to Hope Herr-Cardillo for its pages, to Liz Byer for her careful copyediting, to Katie Monaghan and Lauren Dooley for helping this book find its readers, and to Kathy Belden for her early encouragement.

Thank you to all the booksellers and reps and buyers who put this book in your carts, in your stores, and in the hands of your community. Thank you to the librarians and the teachers, too, who may shelve and share this book—or any book! We writers and readers are lucky to have you in our corner.

Thank you to the writing programs that supported me and introduced me to fiction that expanded my understanding of what a story could and should do. Thank you to the English Department at Mississippi State, especially Tommy Anderson and Mike Kardos. Thank you to the MFA program at Vanderbilt University, especially to Nancy Reisman, Lorrie Moore, and Piyali Bhattacharya for reading the earliest stories in this book. Thank you to my classmates there—for their close-reads, for their friendship and fellowship, and their own beautiful work—especially Jesse Bertron, Rita Bullwinkel, Tiana Clark, Alina Grabowski, Mark Haslam, Sam Rutter, and Anna Silverstein.

And thank you to the writers I've met since—some of whom have edited and nurtured these stories—especially Kayla Kumari Upadhyaya and Rebecca Rubenstein. Big thanks—endless thanks—to Nana Kwame Adjei-Brenyah, who has supported and encouraged me and *House Gone Quiet* every step of the way. And thanks to Tin

House Writers Workshop for bringing us all together. Thank you to the talented and generous writers who offered blurbs, their time, and early support to this book—my forever gratitude goes to you all. Thanks to the story writers who cleared space for a book like this one. Thank you to the Porches Writing Retreat and the American Academy of Arts and Letters. Thank you to Kristina Moore at United Talent Agency.

How do I even say thank you for the rest of it? Here goes it: Thank you to my wonderful extended family and my family of friends. Thank you, Mom and Dad and Dave, for your love, your guidance, and your laughter. This book is nearly as much y'all's doing as it is mine. Thank you to Tula and Mos, even though they can't read. And thank you to Alex, for everything. I would be, both figuratively and literally, lost without you. You're my home— my house gone loud(!). I love you.

ABOUT THE AUTHOR

KELSEY NORRIS is a writer and editor from Alabama. She earned an MFA from Vanderbilt University and has worked as a Peace Corps education volunteer, a school librarian, and a bookseller. Her work has been published in the *Kenyon Review*, *Black Warrior Review*, *Oxford American*, and others. She lives in Washington, DC. For more information, please visit her website at kelseynorris.com.